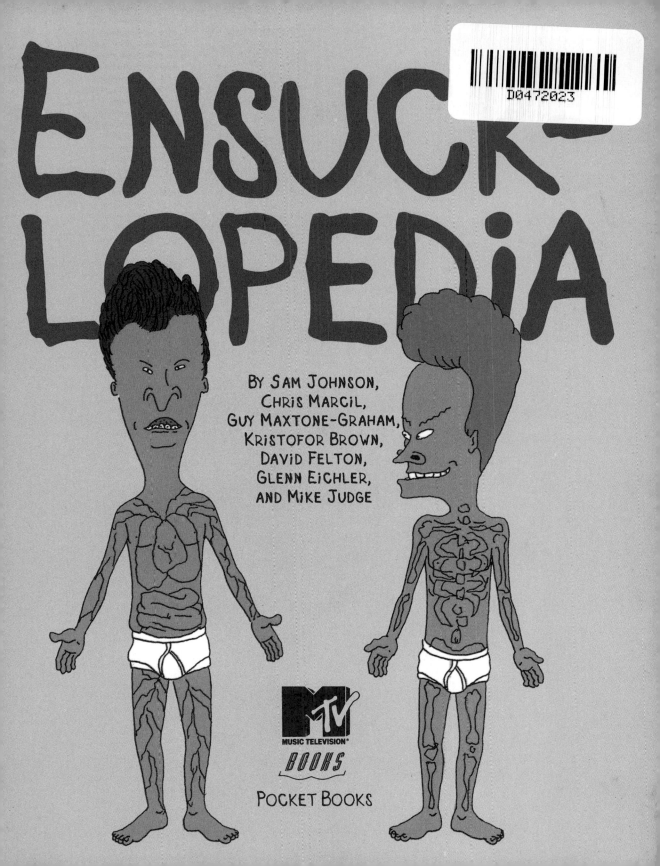

ENSUCK-LOPEDIA

By Sam Johnson,
Chris Marcil,
Guy Maxtone-Graham,
Kristofor Brown,
David Felton,
Glenn Eichler,
and Mike Judge

MTV
MUSIC TELEVISION®
BOOKS
POCKET BOOKS

Beavis and Butt-head are not role models. They're not even human. They're cartoons.
Some of the things they do would cause a real person to get hurt, expelled, arrested, possibly deported.
To put it another way: Don't try this at home.

Editorial Director: Mike Judge
Editor: Glenn Eichler

Art Direction: Roger Gorman, Reiner Design Consultants, Inc.
Illustration Supervisor: Dominie Mahl.
Illustrators: Mike Judge, Kevin Lofton, Miguel Martinez-Joffre, and Bryon Moore
Colorists: Masako Kanayama and Robert Charde

**Special thanks at MTV to: John Andrews, Jonathan Cropper, Howard Handler, Joy Marcus, Jeffrey Marshall, Judy McGrath,
Ed Paparo, Renee Presser, Lisa Silfen, Robin Silverman, Sabrina Silverberg, Donald Silvey, Abby Terkuhle, and Van Toffler**

**Special thanks at Pocket Books to: Lynda Castillo, Gina Centrello, Amy Einhorn, Jack Romanos, Bill Siebert,
Jennifer Weidman, Kara Welsh, and Irene Yuss**

This book is a work of fiction. Names, characters, places and incidents
are either products of the authors' imagination or are used fictitiously.

Cover Illustration from *The Joy of Knowledge* by Mitchell Beazley courtesy of Reed Consumer Books.
Photo credits: Cover photographs, clockwise from top left: Bettmann Archive, Bettmann Archive, Archive Photos, Bettmann
Archive, Bettmann Archive, Archive Photos, Archive Photos, Archive Photos, Archive Photos, Bettmann Archive, Bettmann
Archive, Archive Photos, Archive Photos, Bettmann Archive, Bettmann Archive, Archive Photos, Archive
Photos, Bettmann Archive, Bettmann Archive, Archive Photos, Archive Photos, Bettmann Archive, Archive Photos, Archive
Photos and Bettmann Archive. Interior photos: Frank Micelotta/Retna Ltd.: pp. 16,17; Archive Photos: pp. 15, 27, 28, top
right 33; Bettmann Archive: pp. 26, top right 32, 72, 73, 80; UPI/Bettmann; pp. 8, 9, bottom left 32, far left and insert 33,
42; AP/Wide World Photos: pp. top left 32, bottom right 33, 51, 64, 65; p. 58, from left to right, top row: AP/Wide World
Photos; second row: Bettmann Archive, AP/Wide World Photos, AP/ Wide World Photos; third row: Archive Photos, AP/Wide
World Photos, AP/Wide World Photos; fourth row: AP/Wide World Photos; p. 59: top row: AP/Wide World Photos; second row:
Wide World Photos, Bettmann Archive, AP/Wide World Photos, Archive Photos; third row: AP/Wide World Photos; fourth row:
AP/Wide World Photos, AP/Wide World Photos, AP/Wide World Photos, Reuters/Bettmann,
Bettmann Archive; p 85

An *Original* Publication of MTV Books/Pocket Books

POCKET BOOKS, a division of Simon & Schuster Inc.
1230 Avenue of the Americas, New York, NY 10020

ISBN: 0-671-52149-7

First MTV Books/Pocket Books trade paperback printing December 1994

10 9 8 7 6 5 4 3 2

POCKET and colophon are registered trademarks of
Simon & Schuster Inc.

Printed in the U.S.A.

ABOUT THE AUTHORS

THAT'S BUTT-HEAD. HE'S PRETTY COOL. HE HANGS OUT A LOT AND WATCHES TV. OR ELSE HE CRUISES FOR CHICKS. YOU KNOW, HE JUST KEEPS CHANGING THE CHANNELS AND WHEN A HOT CHICK COMES ON HE'LL CHECK OUT HER THINGIES. IT'S PRETTY COOL. HEY, CHECK THIS OUT. "THE PEN IS MIGHTIER THAN THE SWORD." WAIT. WAIT. "THE PENIS MIGHTIER THAN THE SWORD." THAT'S WHAT I'VE GOT, HEH HEH HEH M HEH. WRITING'S COOL!

UH, THIS IS BEAVIS. HE'S A POET, A STORY-TELLER, A WUSS, A FARTKNOCKER, A DILLWEED, A DOORSTOP AND A PAPERWEIGHT. HUH HUH, AND HE'S A DUMBASS. PLUS HE'S A REAL WUSS. HE'S NEVER GOTTEN ANY. HE LIVES AT HOME WITH NO WIFE AND NO KIDS. JUST HIS PET MONKEY, HUH HUH. BEAVIS HAS WON MANY AWARDS, INCLUDING MY FOOT KICKING HIS ASS AND MY FIST IN HIS FACE. EVEN THOUGH I LET HIM HANG OUT WITH ME, IT DOESN'T MEAN I'M INTERESTED IN DUDES, OR ANYTHING. MOSTLY I JUST KEEP HIM AROUND SO I'LL LOOK EVEN MORE STUDLY AROUND CHICKS. COMPARED TO HIM. BEAVIS, I MEAN.

PRONOUNSIASHUN GUIDE

Ass	"Ass"
Asswipe	"Asswipe"
Uh, anything in Spanish	"Hamana por queno salsa, please"
Dillweed	"Dillhole"
Butt	"But." The second T is silent but deadly, huh huh
Drive through, please	"Riperuebleev"
69	Like it's spelled
The F Word	"Fart"
The S Word	"Sucks"
Boob	If you have to ask, you'll never know
Vulva	Uh, that's some science word, I guess. Ask Daria
Weiner	"Penis," heh heh heh
Beavis	Rhymes with "Weiner"
Hooter	See "Boob." See two of them, if you can. (But, seriously, pronunciate it "thingie" around chicks)

Aa CLASSIFIED ADS

PERSONALS

DO YOUR FRIENDS TEASE YOU...
...Because your thingies are so big? This, like, very sensitive (in more ways than one, huh huh) guy wants to heel your emoshunal wounds, or something. I'll take a hands-on approach to your problem, uh, problems. BOX 69.

YOU: BEAUTIFUL, STACKED MODEL
Me: Handsome sex machine named "Butt-Head." Come to Butt-Head! BOX 69.

OZZY OSBOURNE TYPE
Seeks Christina Apple Gate lookalike. Must know how to rock. And how to do it. Oh yeah, and if, like, you're the real Christina or that Baywatch chick and you're reading this, then you should definitely respond. I'll let you star in some, uh, home movies. Huh huh huh huh. BOX 69.

DO YOU LIKE HOLDING HANDS...
...Walking on the beach under the, huh huh, moon,

PERSONALS

quiet evenings by the fi-- TV, and candlelight dinners? Then don't call, cause we, like, don't have time for any of that crap. Only call if you're, like, interested in doing it and stuff. BOX 69.

SWM, 14
SKS (uh, that stands for "seeks," not "sucks") one SWF 4 SX (that stands for "sex." Heh heh heh). Um, XYZ, PDQ, LMNOP and PB4UGO2BED. BOX 69.

ARE YOU A HOT CHICK?
Two young studs seek hot chicks for, uh, you know, huh huh huh huh. Send a letter and a naked photo. That'd be cool! But don't worry that much about the letter, if your not that good at writing and stuff. Poster-sized would be fine. For the photo, we mean. BOX 69.

ARE YOU A DUDE?
Then quit reading this, fart-knocker! These classified ads are for chicks only. BOX 69.

PERSONALS

FREE LESSONS...
...In, like, how to do it. Only the seriously hot need respond, or something. BOX 69.

WANNA HAVE INTERCOURSE?
You know, like, SEXUAL intercourse? Heh heh heh heh heh! I wrote "sexual intercourse!" BOX 69.

BUSINESS OPPORTUNITIES

MAID WANTED
Must know how to polish wood. Huh huh huh huh. BOX 69.

PETS

ADOPT A MONKEY
Small, friendly, playful monkey, likes to "fetch bones." Heh heh m heh heh heh! Now seeking new owner. Current owner spanks him frequently. Answers to the name of "Little Beavis." BOX 69.

FOR SALE

SPERM
Huh huh huh huh huh. Heh heh heh heh m heh heh heh. Box 69

Aa ANATOMY SECTION

THE HUMAN BUTT, BY BUTT-HEAD

THE BUTT IS THE MOST IMPORTANT PART OF THE BODY. THAT'S HOW COME THE BUTT RULES. GOD GAVE US THE BUTT SO THAT WE COULD, LIKE, HAVE SOMETHING TO TALK ABOUT. THE FIRST BUTT WAS INVENTED LIKE, A LONG TIME AGO BY THE SAME GUY THAT INVENTED THE TOILET. THE BUTT HAS A CRACK IN IT, HUH HUH HUH HUH. GOD PUT A CRACK IN OUR BUTTS SO THAT WE MIGHT HAVE TWO BUTT CHEEKS INSTEAD OF ONE. SOME ANIMALS LIKE FISH DON'T HAVE BUTTS. THAT'S WHY THEY SUCK. OH YEAH, I ALMOST FORGOT, THERE'S ALSO YOUR BUTTHOLE. IT'S LIKE, IN THE MIDDLE. I COULD WRITE A WHOLE BOOK ABOUT THE BUTTHOLE.

HOW THE BUTT WORKS.

INSIDE YOUR BUTT THERE'S ALL THIS COMPLICATED STUFF THAT LIKE, MAKES TURDS HAPPEN. THERE'S ALL THESE TUBES AND STUFF. THEN THE TURDS COME OUT OF YOUR BUTT, HUH HUH. (SEE ALSO: TURDS)

MAKE YOUR OWN BUTT.

YOU CAN MAKE YOUR OWN BUTT AT HOME. YOU GET TWO THINGS THAT ARE LIKE, ROUND AND THEN YOU LIKE, PUT 'EM TOGETHER. HUH HUH HUH. IT LOOKS LIKE A BUTT. CLAY WORKS PRETTY GOOD. YOU CAN ALSO MAKE A FACE OUT OF YOUR BUTT BY DRAWING EYES ON ONE OF YOUR BUTTCHEEKS AND THEN LYING DOWN SIDEWAYS. OH YEAH, YOU HAVE TO PULL DOWN YOUR PANTS FIRST. YOU CAN MAKE A BUTT OUT OF YOUR FACE BY DRAWING A BIG CRACK DOWN THE MIDDLE, HUH HUH. THEN LIKE INSTEAD OF CHEEKS YOU HAVE BUTT CHEEKS. (SEE ALSO: TURDS, MAKING YOUR OWN; PLAYDOUGH, FUN WITH)

OTHER STUFF TO CALL YOUR BUTT.

THE BEST THING TO CALL YOUR BUTT IS YOUR BUTT, BUT SOME PEOPLE LIKE TO CALL IT OTHER STUFF LIKE "ASS" AND "REAR" AND STUFF. WHEN BEAVIS WAS LITTLE, EVERY WEEK AFTER HE TOOK A DUMP HIS MOM USED TO SAY, "AREN'T YOU GLAD TO GET THAT OUT OF YOUR SYSTEM?" SO SOMETIMES WE CALL YOUR BUTT YOUR "SYSTEM," HUH HUH. LIKE, "CHECK IT OUT. YOU CAN SEE HER SYSTEM, HUH HUH HUH."

THE NADS, BY BEAVIS

THE NADS ARE COOL. I LIKE TO TALK ABOUT NADS. NADS. NADS. NADS! INSIDE YOUR NADS THERE'S ALL THESE LIKE, MOLECULES AND STUFF THAT CAUSE ALL THESE COMPLICATED CHEMICALS TO MAKE YOUR WEINER GET BIG WHEN YOU SEE A CHICK. THAT'S HOW COME WHEN THEY CHOP OFF A HORSE'S NADS, IT TURNS INTO A WUSS. SOMETIMES I GET A BONER WHEN I WATCH BAYWATCH. CHEMICALS ARE COOL!

SHUT UP, BEAVIS! YOU'RE NOT TELLING IT RIGHT. THAT'S NOT HOW YOUR NADS WORK. THERE'S ALL THESE TUBES IN YOUR NADS CALLED THE SEMINEFEROUS TUBULES. THEY'RE REALLY IMPORTANT BECAUSE IF YOU DIDN'T HAVE 'EM YOU'D LIKE, NEVER GET MORNING WOOD OR ANYTHING. THEY HOOK UP YOUR WEINER TO YOUR NADS. THEY'RE ALSO HOOKED UP TO YOUR EYES. IF YOU'RE LIKE, WATCHING TV AND YOU SEE A CHICK IN A BIKINI, YOUR EYES TELL YOUR SEMINEFEROUS TUBULES IN YOUR NADS TO MAKE YOUR WEINER GET BIGGER. SOMETIMES THAT HAPPENS TO BEAVIS WHEN HE SEES A DUDE. HUH HUH HUH.

SHUT UP, BUNGHOLE.

THE MUCOUS MEMBRANES

THIS IS THE PART OF YOUR BRAIN THAT MAKES YOU REMEMBER MUCOUS. MUCOUS MEMBRANES ARE REALLY IMPORTANT CAUSE IF YOU DIDN'T HAVE 'EM YOU'D LIKE, FORGET TO PICK YOUR NOSE. THAT'S WHEN YOU GO, LIKE, INSANE IN THE MEMBRANE OR SOMETHING.

THE KERMODIAL BUTTNOIDS

THE GLANDS THAT MAKE YOUR BUTT STINK.

THE FERBICAL NAD CLOBULES

THEY'RE THESE THINGS IN YOUR NADS THAT MAKE IT HURT WHEN SOMONE KICKS YOU IN THE NADS. THEY ALSO MAKE YOUR NADS ITCH. SOMETIMES THEY CRAWL UP INTO YOUR BUTT AND MAKE YOUR BUTT ITCH. HAVING YOUR BUTT ITCH SUCKS, BUT I LIKE SCRATCHING MY BUTT WHEN IT ITCHES. IT'S THE DAMNDEST THING. (SEE ALSO: THE HUMAN BUTT)

THE VIRGINIA

UUUHH...HUH HUH HUH HUH. WE DON'T KNOW MUCH ABOUT THIS.

Bb BACON

CC CREATION (THE STORY OF)

A LONG TIME AGO, LIKE DURING THOSE GIRAFFE PARK TIMES,

THERE WAS THIS DUDE, GOD, AND HE WAS, LIKE, REALLY BIG, AND LIKE, EVERYWHERE,

BUT NOBODY COULD SEE HIM, CAUSE HE WAS LIKE INDIVISIBLE OR SOMETHING.

SO HE COULD, LIKE, GO IN CHICKS' LOCKER ROOMS UNDETECTIVE, EXCEPT THERE

WERE NO CHICKS OR LOCKER ROOMS OR ANYTHING ELSE. THERE.

SO HE SAID, "THIS SUCKS." THEN HE SAID, "LET THERE BE STUFF."

AND LIKE THERE WAS THE EARTH AND STUFF.

AND GOD THOUGHT THE EARTH WAS PRETTY COOL,

BUT STILL NO NAKED CHICKS, SO HE MADE ONE. AND A NAKED DUDE, TOO.

AND THEY, LIKE, DID IT A BUNCH OF TIMES, AND THEY GAVE BIRTH TO ALL THE PEOPLE

IN THE WORLD (SCIENTISTS CALL THIS THE BIG BANG THEORY). BUT THEY

DIDN'T HAVE ENOUGH MONEY TO TAKE CARE OF THEM ALL, SO THEIR KIDS HAD

TO, LIKE, GO TO OTHER COUNTRIES TO FIND JOBS AND STUFF.

BUT BY THEN MONKEYS HAD LEARNED TO USE POWER TOOLS SO LIKE

THEY HAD TO COMPLETE WITH THEM FOR JOBS AND IT WAS HARD.

HUH HUH. HARD. SO THEY DID IT SOME MORE.

Cc CHINA

Beavis is like Chinese food, huh huh! One hour after he spanks his monkey, he's ready again. No way, dillhole! It's more like ten minutes, heh heh.

Huh huh, how did you like the "Sum Yung Gai"? Yeah, heh-heh, how about the "Turd Fried Rice"?

You have mastered the technique of holding your own chopstick, Grasshopper. Huh huh huh, "mastered!"

Parts of this fortune cookie have been recycled by Beavis.

The journey of 1,000 miles starts in my pants.

You will meet a stud named Butt-head. You will give yourself to him. Uh, if you're a chick, that is.

Cc CHICKS

THERE'S THIS JOKE, HUH HUH, ABOUT WHAT THE PERFECT CHICK LOOKS LIKE. IT'S PROBLY PRETTY FUNNY. BUT LIKE, THIS PAGE IS MORE LIKE A SCIENTIFIC GUIDE AND STUFF THAN A JOKE. AND SO YOU CAN GET LIKE THE MOST EXACT IDEA OF WHAT A PERFECT CHICK IS, WE DECIDED TO DRAW IT INSTEAD OF PUTTING A PICTURE HERE AND STUFF. PLUS ALL OUR PICTURES OF PERFECT WOMEN ARE KINDA WRINKLED BY NOW.

HEAD—LIKE, A PERFECT CHICK SHOULD HAVE LIKE A REALLY HOT FACE, BUT LIKE, DON'T WORRY ABOUT IT CAUSE THAT'S LIKE THE LEAST IMPORTANT PART OF ANY CHICK CAUSE LIKE YOU CAN ALWAYS WEAR A BAG ON YOUR HEAD, HUH HUH. BUT LIKE, IN THE HEAD AREA, IT'S BETTER IF A CHICK HAS A PERFECT FACE THAN LIKE, A PERFECT BRAIN? CAUSE THEN SHE STARTS THINKING STUFF AND SAYING JUNK LIKE, "QUIT LOOKING AT MY THINGIES." IF A CHICK STARTS TALKING A BUNCH A CRAP LIKE THAT, IT'S LIKE A SIGN SHE MIGHT NOT BE PERFECT.

THINGIES—A CHICK SHOULD HAVE REALLY BIG THINGIES, BUT NOT SO BIG THAT IT'S LIKE SICK OR SOMETHING. ACTUALLY THAT WOULD BE OK. BUT AT LEAST MAKE SURE THEY'RE ATTACHED TO A CHICK, AND NOT LIKE THE THINGIES THAT FAT DUDES HAVE AT THE BEACH. ONE TIME BEAVIS TRIED TO COP A FEEL OFF A FAT DUDE AT THE BEACH AND LIKE, THE DUDE KICKED THE CRAP OUT OF HIM. HUH HUH. HE WAS FAST FOR A FAT DUDE.

HIPS AND BUTT-AL AREA—LIKE, A CHICK SHOULD BE CURVY HERE. IF YOU ASK YOURSELF, UH, IS SHE CURVY ENOUGH? AND YOU CAN'T DECIDE THE ANSWER, THINK OF LIKE ONE A THOSE GLASS THINGS WITH SAND IN IT THAT'S SPOSED TO KEEP TIME. I THINK IT'S CALLED A SAND WATCH OR SOMETHING. EXCEPT PUT EYES AND LIKE HAIR ON THE TOP, AND LIKE SKIN INSTEAD OF GLASS, AND LIKE BLOOD AND INTESTINES AND CRAP INSTEAD OF SAND. IF THE CHICK YOU'RE LOOKING AT KIND OF LOOKS LIKE THAT, AND SHE HASN'T LIKE CALLED THE COPS YET OR ANYTHING, THEN YOU CAN SAY, "NICE BUTT, HUH HUH" AND REALLY MEAN IT. CHICKS LIKE IT WHEN YOU SAY STUFF LIKE THAT AND YOU'RE NOT LYING. IT'S CALLED SINCERENESS.

LEGS—LEGS HAVE TO BE GOOD-SHAPED, AND LIKE, LONG. BUT IF THE CHICK IS SHORT, AND HER LEGS CAN'T BE LONG, THEN THAT'S OK TOO, AS LONG AS THEY'RE GOOD-SHAPED. ALSO, SHE SHOULD SHAVE THEM, BUT LIKE, WE'RE TALKING ABOUT WOMEN ANYWAY, AND NOT LIKE A COLLEGE CHICK WHO WALKS AROUND WITH LIKE HAIRY LEGS AND BOOKS AND STUFF.

SHOES—WE ALMOST FORGOT CLOTHES SO WE'RE GONNA TALK ABOUT IT HERE. BUT SINCE THIS IS LIKE THE PERFECT WOMAN, WE'RE GONNA FORGET THE CLOTHES AFTER ALL. HUH HUH HUH HUH.

SO LIKE, THAT'S THE PERFECT WOMAN. IF YOU'RE GOING LIKE, "WHOA, WHAT ABOUT OTHER STUFF, LIKE PERSONALITY OR SOMETHING," DON'T BE, CAUSE IN OUR SCIENTIFIC OPINION AS DUDES, A CHICK ONLY GETS A PERSONALITY IF SHE'S UH, UNPERFECT, JUST LIKE THE WAY A DUDE WHO CAN'T KICK PEOPLE'S ASSES WILL LIKE DO HOMEWORK AND STUFF. IT'S CALLED EVERLOTION OR SOMETHING.

CC CORRESPONDENCE

Keep The Tip, Huh Huh

I never thought this letter was true until it happened to me, or something. One time I was at the arcade at the mall and there was this really hot chick playing the video game next to me. She was, like, really well built, with two thingies and stuff? Oh yeah, she had brown hair. Or maybe she was blonde, or a redhead, I forget. Maybe she was bald, huh huh huh. But she did have two thingies, I remember those pretty well.

Anyway, she dropped her quarter on the ground and as she bent down I could tell she was, like, trying to give me a good peek at her ample thingies. Quick as a flash, I stepped on her quarter and gave her a look that said, "Come to Butt-Head!"

She was getting pretty hot and bothered. Really, you know, wanting to get her quarter back. I was, like, thinking about taking the quarter and dropping it down my pants. Huh huh, that woulda been cool! Then, with this really sexy smile and thingies that were still pretty big, she said, "Move your foot, you moron, or my boyfriend will kick your ass."

I've never seen her since, but I'll always remember that special time we shared together and stuff. She wanted it.
—*Name and address withheld.*

She Wears A Bra

Eh, heh heh, there's this chick in my class? And I like to stare at her, and stuff. She must not mind, cause she'll just sit there when I'm staring at her, and pretend not to notice. She looks really hot! That's just, you know, judging from the back of her head. I bet the rest of her is pretty hot, too.

She must be pretty stacked, cause if you look really closely at the back of her shirt, you can tell she wears a bra. You can see all the wires and pulleys and stuff through her shirt.

Heh heh m heh. "Pulleys!" Um, "Pull these!" Heh heh heh. "Pull these, puh-lease!" That would be cool! —*Name and address withheld.*

School's Hard

Uh, there's this chick in our class. Beavis really wants her and stuff, even though she doesn't know he exists. And even if she knew he exists, she probably wouldn't like him, cause then she'd know what a wuss he is, huh huh huh!

Anyway, one day Beavis was, uh, looking at her a little too long? Then Van Driessen asked him to come up to the front of the class to write something on the blackboard. Huh huh huh huh, he had a stiffy!

So Beavis, like, wouldn't go up to the blackboard. And when Van Driessen asked him why not, he said, "Uh, because I have an erection."

Huh huh huh huh huh, what a dumbass! He probably could have gone up to the blackboard anyway, and people wouldn't have noticed, cause his weiner's pretty small. Everybody laughed at him, including the chick he'd been staring at. Beavis spent the rest of the day in the school psychoticist's office. I don't even think this chick is very hot.—*Name and address withheld.*

Mom Yes, Apple Pie No.

Uh, I had sex once? With Beavis's mom, huh huh huh.

Shut up, fartknocker.—*Name and address withheld.*

French Lessons

Eh, heh heh, I was, like, hanging out in my dorm room late Monday night when --

Beavis, you dumbass, you weren't in a dorm room. You were sitting on the couch watching "Baywatch."

No way. I was in, like, a dorm room studying for, like a big French exam or something, when all of a sudden I heard this knocking sound.

That was the sound of me hitting you on the head, dumbass.

No way! It was like this really stacked French chick. And she said she was there to help me study for my exam, by, like doing it with me. Heh heh heh.

Beavis, you've never even met any French chicks. Except for Madame Palm and her five daughters, huh huh huh. All that happened on Monday is you saw "Baywatch" and then you spanked your monkey.

Oh yeah.—*Name, address and weiner withheld.*

1. STAGE. THIS IS THE PLACE WHERE, LIKE, IT ALL HAPPENS OR SOMETHING. LIKE, THE FAT DUDE IN CROWBAR COMES UP TO THE FRONT HERE, AND SQUATS DOWN AND STARTS GROANING. THAT'S WHEN IT'S LIKE, MAGIC TIME OR WHATEVER.

2. SPEAKERS. THIS IS WHAT THE MUSIC SHOOTS OUT OF. IT'S LIKE, THERE'S TWO KINDS OF MUSIC: LOUD AND SUCKY. YOU NEVER HEAR SUCKY MUSIC AT CONCERTS, UNLESS YOU GOT RIPPED OFF, OR IT'S, UH, JAZZ OR SOMETHING. LOUD MUSIC SHOOTS OUT INTO THE AIR AND RIGHT INTO YOUR BRAIN, HUH HUH. AND LIKE, EVERYTHING SHAKES AND STUFF, EVEN YOUR BRAIN. YOUR WHOLE BODY'S SHAKING AND VIBRATING AND WHATEVER, AND IT'S LIKE THAT SAYING OF HOW YOU CAN'T EVEN HEAR YOURSELF THINK. BUT IT'S LIKE, SO WHAT. THINKING'S A PAIN IN THE ASS ANYWAY. HUH HUH. ASS. PLUS BEAVIS LIKES IT CAUSE HE CAN'T HEAR ANY OF THE OTHER DUDES WHO LIVE IN HIS HEAD EITHER.

3. SECURITY GUARDS. THERE'S ALL THESE DUDES HERE IN FRONT OF THE STAGE WHO LIKE TALK TO EACH OTHER WITH WALKIE-TALKIES AND STUFF. THEY'RE LIKE, UH, STRIKER UNIT 12, WE GOT A SITUATION IN BAKER SECTOR, OVER. HUH HUH. GET THE HELL BACK FROM THE STAGE DAMMIT OR I'LL SPLIT YOUR HEAD LIKE A HALLOWEEN PUMPKIN. THESE DUDES WOULD BE JUST NORMAL ASSWIPES EXCEPT THAT THEY GO TO MORE CONCERTS THAN ANYBODY. SO THAT MAKES THEM A LITTLE HIGHER UP THAN JUST NORMAL ASSWIPES.

4. BACKSTAGE. MEMBER HOW I SAID IT ALL HAPPENS ON THE STAGE? UH, WELL, LIKE SOME OTHER STUFF HAPPENS OVER HERE, BACKSTAGE. THEY HAVE FOOD, AND BEERS, UNLESS IT'S ONE A THOSE BANDS THAT HAD TO BUST THEMSELVES CAUSE THEY GOT MESSED UP ON BEERS AND STUFF. THEY HAVE SLUSHIES OR SOMETHING, I GUESS. AND THIS IS WHERE OZZY KEEPS ALL THE ANIMALS AND STUFF THAT HE'S GONNA BITE THE HEADS OFF OF DURING THE SHOW. AND LIKE, THIS IS WHERE ALL THE UH, HUH HUH, CHICKS LEAVE THEIR BOYFRIENDS BEFORE GETTING ON THE BAND BUS SO THEY CAN DO IT. UH, YOU CAN'T SEE THE BUS ON THIS PICTURE CAUSE UH, I THINK THE DRIVER WENT OVER TO THE HINKY DINKY TO PICK UP SOME COLESLAW OR SOMETHING. FOR THE CHICKS.

5. LIGHT BOARD. THERE'S THIS BIG TABLE THING AT THE BACK HERE AND IT'S GOT ALL THESE KNOBS ON IT AND CRAP, AND LIKE, A BUNCH A WIRES IN IT. IT CONTROLS ALL THE LECTRICITY AND STUFF. AND THERE'S THIS BIG FAT DUDE WHO SITS THERE AND LIKE, DOESN'T EVEN LISTEN TO THE MUSIC HARDLY, HE JUST MESSES WITH THE KNOBS AND TELLS PEOPLE HE'S GONNA COME DOWN AND KICK THEIR ASS IF THEY DON'T QUIT LEANING AGAINST THE BOARD. HUH HUH. I THINK HE'S, UH, SCARED CAUSE OF THE LECTRICITY. BUT IT'S LIKE BEAVIS TOOK A WHIZ ON SOME LECTRICAL WIRES ONE TIME AND IT JUST LIKE, TURNED HIS WEINER BLACK FOR A COUPLE WEEKS.

6. MOSH PIT. THIS PLACE ROCKS. IT'S LIKE, PEOPLE HITTING YOU AND PUSHING YOU AND JUMPING ON YOUR NECK AND KICKING YOUR FACE AND HITTING YOUR HEAD WITH THEIR KNEES AND KNOCKING YOU ON THE GROUND AND STOMPING ON YOUR NADS AND FALLING ON TOP OF YOU AND ELBOWING YOUR CHEST AND STUFF. IT'S LIKE A BIG, COOL FAMILY.

7. TEE-SHIRT SELLERS. IF I WAS SMART, I'D LIKE GO DOWN TO THE ST. VINCENT OF PAUL AND BUY ALL THE OLD USED TEE SHIRTS FOR ABOUT A PENNY AND THEN LIKE WRITE GWAR ON THEM AND SELL THEM AT A GWAR CONCERT FOR 50 BUCKS. HUH HUH. IT'S A TOTAL RIPOFF AND STUFF. GOOD THING I'M NOT SMART OR I'D PROBLY BE RIPPING YOU OFF RIGHT NOW.

8. BEACH BALL. BEFORE THE CONCERT, PEOPLE ARE LIKE, WE HAVE NERVOUS ENERGY OR SOMETHING, WE NEED TO BE ZAPPED BY HIGH-INTENSITY SOUND. OR THEY'RE LIKE, THE OPENING ACT SUCKS. SO THEY THROW A BEACH BALL AROUND SOMETIMES, OR ONE A THOSE FRISBEES OR A GLOW STICK. ONE TIME BEAVIS TRIED TO GET PEOPLE TO THROW AROUND THIS FLAT EMPTY COFFEE CAN HE PICKED UP OFF THE HIGHWAY. I GUESS THEY WERE LIKE, TOO EXCITED CAUSE, LIKE, NOBODY THREW IT BACK AFTER WE CHUCKED IT REAL HARD INTO THE PIT. IT WAS STILL A PRETTY GOOD IDEA. FOR BEAVIS.

9. DANCING CHICK. THERE'S USUALLY A CHICK RIGHT OVER HERE WHO LIKE SWAYS BACK AND FORTH AND SPINS AROUND LIKE SHE'S LISTENING TO DIFFERENT MUSIC FROM WHAT EVERYBODY ELSE IS. LISTENING TO. AND THEN YOU GO OVER AND GO LIKE, HEY BABY. AND SHE KEEPS DANCING AND STUFF AND ACTING LIKE YOU'RE NOT EVEN THERE. AND THEN YOU GO, LET'S GET IT ON, FOX. AND SHE KEEPS DANCING. AND THEN YOU'RE LIKE, OKAY, FORGET YOU. THERE'S OTHER CHICKS IN THE SEA.

10. STAIN. USUALLY THERE'S A STAIN OVER HERE. AND YOUR FEET STICK ON IT. IT COULD BE LIKE, SOMEBODY'S DRINK, OR LIKE SOME PUKE OR SOMETHING. OR IT COULD BE BLOOD OR LIKE A DEAD ANIMAL. IN THE END, YOU NEVER FIND OUT WHAT IT IS, AND YOU STOP THINKING ABOUT IT. BUT WHEN YOU WERE THINKING ABOUT IT, IT WAS COOL.

CC BUTT-HEAD'S REPORT CARD

GRADE REPORT

HIGHLAND HIGH

(A=Excellent; B=Outstanding; C=Above Average; D=Good; F=Not Very Good*)

STUDENT NAME: *Butt-head*   GRADE: N/A

Language Arts   F   D   C-   F
Inner conflict, self-esteem problems prevent full self-expression—DVD

> UH, THIS WOULD BE COOL IF THEY TALKED ENGLISH OR SOMETHING.

Introduction to Business Arts   D-   F   D   B-
"Butt-O-Gram" marketing project a stroke of adequacy—MW

> I PUT THE BUTT IN PEOPLE'S BIRTHDAYS. BUSINESS IS COOL.

Science Arts   D   D   D-   D
HAS BEEN INTERESTING TEST SUBJECT; OTHERWISE A WASTE OF A ZYGOTE—SJK

> I CHECKED IF EVERYTHING WAS, YOU KNOW, "ANATOMICALLY CORRECT."

Math I   C-   D   D-   F
Must learn to stop laughing at the word "algebra"—DVD

> HUH HUH HUH HUH HUH.

Basic Hygiene   F   F   F   F
This student is a maggot—BB

> IF GOD WANTED ME TO WASH, HE WOULDA MADE ME SMELL LIKE A SHOWER, OR SOMETHING.

Beginning Spanish   D   D   D   F
Debe morir Butt-head—JST

> LO SUCKO MI POCHO HAMANA HAMANA TO YOU TOO, DILLWEED.

Physical Education   D   D   D   D
Figure of ridicule is all the figure he'll ever have—BB

> THIS WAS THE CLASS WHERE THEY KEPT ASKING THE TRICK QUESTIONS, I THINK.

Socio-Cultural Studies   C   C   C   C
Excellent attendance!—DVD

> VAN DRIESSEN SAID I MISUNDERSTOOD OTHER CULTURES JUST THE SAME AS MY OWN.

*As the result of a recent court ruling, the meaning of the "F" grade has been changed from the pejorative term "Fail" to the stern but less emotionally damaging "Not Very Good." Some parents may also want to implement their own "curve" to compensate for any regrettable but unavoidable Western European ethnocentrism which may have occured in class.

DREAMS and

DREAMS ARE COOL, CAUSE IT'S LIKE YOU'RE STILL WATCHING TV EVEN THOUGH YOU'RE SLEEPING. THE ONLY THING THAT SUCKS ABOUT THEM IS WAKING UP. SOMETIMES YOU HAVE TO GO BACK AND SLEEP ALL DAY, JUST TO FINISH A DREAM. BUT, LIKE, WHATEVER IT TAKES OR SOMETHING.

SOME DUDE ON TV SAID YOUR DREAMS ARE SPOSED TO MEAN SOMETHING. LIKE, IF YOU KILLED A BUNCH OF BUGS DURING THE DAY, THAT NIGHT YOU MIGHT DREAM ABOUT KILLING A BUNCH OF BUGS. SO WE, LIKE, DECIDED TO ANALEYES SOME OF OUR COOLEST DREAMS.

BUTT-HEAD'S DREAM: SO LIKE, I HAVE THIS ONE WHERE I GO OVER TO BEAVIS'S HOUSE, AND I JUST WALK IN, BUT I CAN'T FIND BEAVIS ANYWHERE. BUT THE BATHROOM DOOR'S OPEN AND I CAN SEE BEAVIS'S MOM, AND SHE'S EATING BANANAS IN THE BATHTUB. SO I'M STANDING THERE, CHECKING OUT HER WET THINGIES AND THINKING THIS IS COOL, WHEN SHE TURNS TO ME AND ASKS ME TO WASH HER BACK. BUT INSTEAD, I SAY I HAVE TO PEE. AND SHE SAYS 'THAT'S NICE.' AND THIS IS THE WEIRD PART... WHEN I WAKE UP AFTER THE DREAM, I HAVE A STIFFY, AND I REALLY HAVE TO PEE.

BEAVIS' ANAL-EYESEES: HMM... THAT'S WEIRD. I WONDER WHERE I WAS?

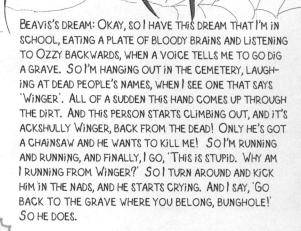

BEAVIS'S DREAM: OKAY, SO I HAVE THIS DREAM THAT I'M IN SCHOOL, EATING A PLATE OF BLOODY BRAINS AND LISTENING TO OZZY BACKWARDS, WHEN A VOICE TELLS ME TO GO DIG A GRAVE. SO I'M HANGING OUT IN THE CEMETERY, LAUGH-ING AT DEAD PEOPLE'S NAMES, WHEN I SEE ONE THAT SAYS 'WINGER'. ALL OF A SUDDEN THIS HAND COMES UP THROUGH THE DIRT. AND THIS PERSON STARTS CLIMBING OUT, AND IT'S ACKSHULLY WINGER, BACK FROM THE DEAD! ONLY HE'S GOT A CHAINSAW AND HE WANTS TO KILL ME! SO I'M RUNNING AND RUNNING, AND FINALLY, I GO, 'THIS IS STUPID. WHY AM I RUNNING FROM WINGER?' SO I TURN AROUND AND KICK HIM IN THE NADS, AND HE STARTS CRYING. AND I SAY, 'GO BACK TO THE GRAVE WHERE YOU BELONG, BUNGHOLE!' SO HE DOES.

BUTT-HEAD'S ANAL-EYESEES: WHOA! THAT'S PRETTY COOL. I GUESS WINGER'S A BIGGER WUSS THAN WE THOUGHT! HUH-HUH HUH.

Nightmares

BEAVIS'S DREAM: SOMETIMES I HAVE THIS DREAM WHERE I GO DOWN INTO THE BASEMENT AND A GIANT SPIDER WITH A FLAMING SKULL HEAD CATCHES ME IN HIS WEB. AND JUST AS HE'S GONNA EAT ME, I WHIP OUT A NAIL GUN AND START SHOOTING HIM IN THE NADS. AND ALL THIS GREEN STUFF STARTS POURING OUT OF HIS GUTS, AND THEN ABOUT TWO THOUSAND BABY SPIDERS COME RUNNING OUT. BUT I DON'T HAVE ENOUGH NAILS TO KILL THEM ALL. BUT IT'S OKAY, CAUSE THE BABY SPIDERS START EATING THE BIG SPIDER AND IN BETWEEN BITES THEY LOOK AT ME AND SAY 'THANKS, BEAVIS.' SO I WATCH THEM FOR A WHILE AND THINK 'THIS IS COOL,' UNTIL I FALL ASLEEP IN THE WEB. AND THEN I USUALLY WAKE UP IN MY BED THE NEXT MORNING, AND THERE'S A BUNCH OF SNOT ON MY PILLOW AND STUFF.

BUTT-HEAD'S ANAL-EYESEES: HUH HUH HUH... YOU'RE A DUMBASS!

BUTT-HEAD'S DREAM: SO LIKE, SOMETIMES I DREAM THAT I'M ABOUT TO DO IT WITH A CHICK, BUT I CAN HEAR BEAVIS IN THE OTHER ROOM, LAUGHING REALLY HARD... AND IT'S PISSING ME OFF, BECAUSE HE'S EITHER LAUGHING AT ME, OR ELSE I'M MISSING SOMETHING REALLY COOL ON TV. SO I TELL THE CHICK I'LL BE RIGHT BACK... AND WHEN I GET TO THE LIVING ROOM BEAVIS IS DEAD. BUT THERE'S A PRETTY COOL SHOW ON TV.

BEAVIS' ANAL-EYESEES: WHAT DO YOU MEAN I'M DEAD?! HOW DO YOU KNOW I WASN'T FAKING IT?
CAUSE YOU WERE DEAD.
NO I WASN'T.
YES YOU WERE.
DON'T MAKE ME KICK YOUR ASS, BUTT-HEAD!
YOU CAN'T KICK MY ASS. YOU'RE DEAD.

BEAVIS'S DREAM: OH YEAH? WELL SOMETIMES I HAVE A DREAM WHERE I KILL BUTT-HEAD, AND HE'S DEAD.

BUTT-HEAD'S ANAL-EYESEES: UHH... THIS MEANS BEAVIS IS A LIAR. HUH HUH. THE END.
NO WAY! WE'RE NOT DONE!
YES WE ARE. HUH HUH.
CUT IT OUT, BUTT-HEAD! I'VE GOT A LOT MORE DREAMS! I GOT DREAMS ABOUT SNAKES AND VAMPIRE BATS AND FOREIGNERS AND GWAR...
DEAD PEOPLE DON'T DREAM, DILLHOLE.
I'M NOT DEAD!!!
OH YEAH? WELL, I GUESS WE'LL JUST HAVE TO WAIT AND SEE IF YOU WAKE UP TOMORROW. HUH HUH. GOOD NIGHT, BEAVIS. I'M GOING TO BED. HUH HUH HUH.

Dd SELF-DEFENSE

UM, LIKE, GETTING YOUR ASS KICKED ALL THE TIME SUCKS, HEH HEH. IT'S LIKE, YOU GOTTA TEACH YOUR ASS TO KICK BACK. YOU GOTTA LEARN TO SELF-DEFEND YOURSELF. HEH HEH. THAT'S WHAT I'M GONNA TEACH YOU HOW TO DO. AND LIKE, YOU GOTTA DO EVERYTHING I SAY BECAUSE I'M NOT ALWAYS GONNA BE AROUND TO HAUL YOUR ASS INTO THE FIRE OR WHATEVER. HEH HEH.

THE BASIC STANCE

UM, FIRST, YOU GOTTA LEARN THE RIGHT WAY TO STAND. STAND LIKE THIS, WITH TWO FEET ON THE GROUND. THAT'S LIKE, THE BEST WAY TO STAND. IT'S EASY, AND UM, PRETTY COMFERBAL. PLUS, IF YOU HAVE TO LIKE FALL DOWN OR SOMETHING, YOU'RE ALREADY STANDING UP, SO YOU'RE IN THE PERFECT POSITION.

THE NAD KICK

LIKE THIS IS THE MOVE THAT LIKE, MY WHOLE SELF-DEFENSE PROGRAM IS BASED ON. IT'S JUST A QUICK KICK MOTION DIRECTLY TO THE NADS. HEH HEH HEH. REALLY FAST AND REALLY HARD. RIGHT IN THE NADS, HEH HEH HEH. JUST MAKE SURE YOU ALWAYS TRY TO GET INTO FIGHTS WITH PEOPLE WHO HAVE NADS.

PLAY DEAD

SOMETIMES, IF YOU, LIKE, IGNORE A PROBLEM, IT GOES AWAY. SO LIKE, IF YOU SUDDENLY PLAY DEAD WHILE SOMEBODY'S KICKING YOUR ASS, THEY'LL LIKE GO AWAY. SOMETIMES.

THE LOOGIE HOCK

UM , EVEN IF LIKE, YOUR ASS HAS BEEN KICKED ALREADY,
YOU CAN SELF-DEFEND YOURSELF HOURS, EVEN UM, DAYS
LATER. YOU JUST HOCK A LOOGIE INTO THE PERSON
WHO KICKED YOUR ASS'S CUP. HEH HEH HEH. THERE'S
ANOTHER MOVE THAT'S A LOT LIKE THIS MOVE, BUT
DIFFERENT, KNOWN AS THE CUP A WHIZ, HEH HEH.

THE STOMP

IF YOU HAVE TO SELF-
DEFEND YOURSELF AGAINST
LIKE, BUGS AND STUFF, OR
LIKE ONE OF THOSE
FLOWERS THAT'S GOT
POINTY THINGS ON IT, OR
LIKE A GUY WHO'S ALREADY
DOWN ON THE GROUND,
YOU CAN DO THE STOMP.
HEH HEH. IT REALLY HURTS,
HEH HEH.

FRIENDSHIP

AFTER YOU'VE LIKE SELF-DEFENDED YOURSELF, TRY TO
BE FRIENDS WITH THE PERSON. THAT WAY THEY WON'T
WANT TO KICK YOUR ASS AGAIN AND YOU CAN LIKE,
JUST GET ON WITH YOUR LIFE. PUT IT ALL BEHIND YOU.
HEH HEH HEH HEH. GET ON. BEHIND.

A Typical Self-Defence Snario

"The Basic Stance"
BUTT-HEAD: "GIMME THAT FROG, ASSWIPE. NOW. HUH HUH."
BEAVIS: "NO WAY, BUNGHOLE."

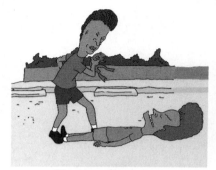

"Playing Dead"
BUTT-HEAD: "YOU WUSS. I BARELY TOUCHED YOU. HUH HUH. MY FROG, NOW."

"The Nad Kick"
BUTT-HEAD: "AAAAAAGH!"
BEAVIS: "M HEH HEH HEH HEH. ASSWIPE."

"The Stomp"
BEAVIS: "GIMME SOME A YOUR SLUSHY, YOU WUSS. HEH HEH HEH. WUSS."
BUTT-HEAD: "UH HUH HUH OW HUH OW."

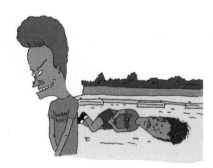

"The Cup a Whiz"
BEAVIS: "HEH HEH HEH HEH M HEH HEH."
BUTT-HEAD: "UUGH. GET OVER HERE AND HELP ME, ASSWIPE."

"Friendship"
BUTT-HEAD: "BEAVIS, AS SOON AS MY NADS FEEL BETTER I'M GONNA BEAT THE CRAP OUT OF YOU."
BEAVIS: "HEH HEH HEH. DRINK THIS—YOU'LL FEEL LOTS BETTER. HEH HEH HEH."

DAHMER, JEFFREY – Uh, I heard he, like, sold arms to the military, or something, huh huh huh! Some dude's arms, I mean. Oh yeah, and he's like really smart, cause he's got lotsa brains, heh heh. You know, like, other people's brains? Huh huh, yeah. And that dude has more guts than anybody else, but he couldn't outrun the cops cause he's got two left feet. And they had trouble taking his fingerprints cause he's all thumbs. And then his lawyer cost him, like, a leg and an arm. Plus a head and two nads, huh huh. Wait, I got one, Butt-Head! Now he's, like, pissed cause the cafeteria in jail doesn't serve chicks' fingers, heh heh heh. That's pretty gross, Beavis. Oh. Oh yeah.

DAMME, VAN – This guy kicks ass. He knows karate stuff, and like, how to kill people, and the stuff he doesn't know, like English, makes him even cooler. Cause when movie dudes know English, they just sit around and talk and cry and stuff instead of getting to the business at hand, which is kicking ass. But as long as Van Damme still speaks European, everything should be cool.

DENADULATION – This chick cut off this guy's thingie, and the guy had to show up and blame her, right on TV. And all through the trial they kept saying "penis." "When did you cut off his penis?" "Is that where the penis was found?" "Is this a photograph of your penis?" Now whenever you see that guy's picture on TV, like on the news or on Renaldo, it says underneath his picture, "WIFE CUT OFF HIS PENIS." And whenever he goes into a restaurant, people say, "There's that dork whose wife cut off his dork." And when people ask him for an autograph, he writes, "Best of luck to Betsy. Signed, the guy whose wife cut off his penis." They should write a book about his life and call it "Where's Woodrow?" Huh huh huh huh. That would be cool.

DESERT NAM – The first war so cool they put the whole thing on TV. There was, like, this Sodomy Insane dude trying to muscle in on our chick, Kuwait? So we kicked his ass. It was cool, cause every time the army fired a shot that hit, they'd make a music video about it and show it on CNN. Plus the reporter dude was like a werewolf. He ruled.

DICK – A wussy dude's name. It's short for "Richard." And Beavis.

DILLHOLE – (See Beavis. Huh huh huh huh)

DILLWEED – (Um, look at Butt-Head. Heh heh m heh heh)

DOG – How come some asswipes have a big ugly dog at home that doesn't even wear clothes and walks around naked all day exposing its weiner and licking its nads. And they feed it steaks and call it their best friend and say "Good doggie," whenever it takes a crap in someone else's yard. But if that same dog was me or Beavis, they'd smack us silly and make us see a counselor? Next time some buttmunch has a "talk" with you, just say, "Hey, why don't you get Rover some pants and maybe he'll stop making a popsicle out of his own butt!"

DOLPHIN – This fish with a hole in its head that likes to eat balloons and stuff. The dolphin likes to eat balloons and stuff, I mean. I don't know what the hole likes to eat. Sometimes tunas get caught in the nets fishing dudes leave out for dolphins, which really sucks, cause tuna fish tastes pretty gross.

DOPPLER EFFECT – The Doppler Effect was named after this dork named Doppler who went around naming stuff so people would think he was a scientist. Sometimes when Beavis farts, it makes a little brown stain in his underpants. I'm going to name that the Butt-Head Effect, and then I'll, you know, get some.

DOUCHE – A feminine hiding product, or something.

DUMBASS – Uh, you should be able to do this one, Beavis, huh huh huh. Um, okay Butt-Head. Eh, heh heh, a dumbass is defined as, um, you know, a dumbass? It's just, like, someone whose butt is as smart as his brain, or something? You know, like a dumbass. This is hard.

Dd DUDES AND CHICKS

THERE'S LIKE TWO DIFFERENT KINDS OF PEOPLE IN THE WORLD, DUDES AND CHICKS, EXCEPT FOR THIS ONE DUDE WE SAW AT THE STATE FAIR WHO'S LIKE A DUDE AND A CHICK, HUH HUH. ME AND BEAVIS ARE DUDES, SO LIKE, WE KNOW A LOT ABOUT LIKE WHAT DUDES THINK ABOUT AND STUFF. HUH HUH. MOSTLY, WE THINK ABOUT CHICKS, SO I GUESS THAT MAKES US EXPERTS ON THEM, TOO. HERE'S SOME A THE STUFF WE KNOW.

A DUDE'S BRAIN IS LIKE DESIGNED FOR COMPLICATED STUFF LIKE SCIENCE. LIKE, FOR COUNTING BEERS AND EXPERIMENTING ON BUGS OR WHATEVER.

A CHICK'S BRAIN IS BUILT TO THINK ABOUT SIMPLER STUFF, LIKE ME AND BEAVIS. HUH HUH. AT ALL TIMES.

THESE ROCK-SOLID MUSCULAR MAN ARMS ARE USED FOR KICKING THE ASSES OF DUDES WHO LOOK AT MY WOMAN.

CHICK ARMS ARE BUILT FOR HOLDING ME, AND LIKE, CARRYING STUFF TO ME. NACHOS AND CRAP.

CHICKS HAVE THESE THINGIES THAT STICK OUT. IT'S LIKE, THEY EVOLUTIONED AFTER CHICKS STARTED WEARING BRAS. IT WAS LIKE, I LIKE MY BRA, BUT IT'S ALL LOOSE AND STUFF. I KNOW, I'LL GROW SOME THINGIES! HUH HUH.

THIS IS A DUDE'S PACKAGE. HUH HUH HUH. IT'S LIKE WHERE HE GETS MOST OF HIS IDEAS FROM.

A DUDE NEEDS PERFECT LEGS LIKE THESE FOR RUNNING AFTER CHICKS AND STUFF. AND LIKE, KICKING OTHER DUDES IN THE NADS, LIKE BEAVIS, HUH HUH.

A CHICK'S LEGS ARE SPOSED TO WORK CLOSELY WITH HER ARMS TO HELP CARRY MY STUFF TO ME. IF THEY WON'T COOPERATE, THE CHICK SHAVES THEM AS PUNISHMENT.

How To Like Talk To A Chick

Sometimes it's hard talking to a chick. Heh heh heh heh heh heh. But, like with chicks? It's like, they say stuff, and like, you have to think of what to say back, and by then they're already getting in some dude's car instead of yours just because he, like, has a car. Here's like some tips on how to like get a chick's attention and then hold it. Heh heh heh. Hold it.

* First, unzip your pants a little bit. Like halfway. That's so, like, the chicks you're talking to will start to, uh, unconshusly think about them. Your pants.

* Like, every time you're about to say something, open your mouth really wide and lick your lips, heh heh. It's a chick turn- on.

* When you first meet a chick, say something that like, shows you like really care about them or whatever.

Something like, "I think I can see your nipple." Heh heh. That's called a ice breaker.

* Sometimes, like, a joke can break the ice too. Something like, "It looked so nice out today I'm not wearing pants." Heh heh. Or like, that one about the dude who goes like I can't hear you cause I got a banana in my rear. Heh heh heh.

* When the conversation dies down, change the subject. Go, "Uh, do you wanna go do it somewhere?" That way there's like, no awkward silences and stuff.

* After about a minute or something, when you've said all there is to say, that's when you make your move. You should try to talk to chicks near where there's a clock so you know when a minute's up. Heh heh. Up.

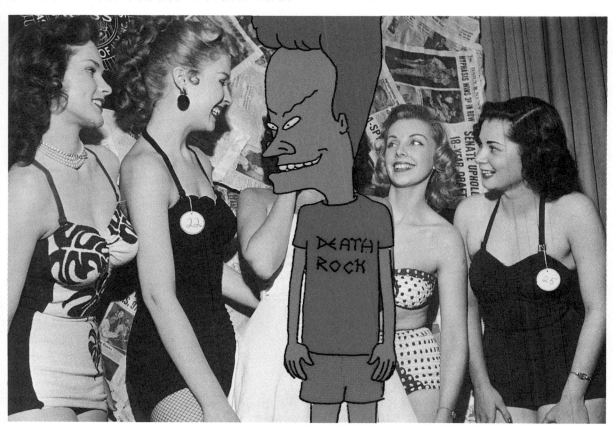

HOW TO GET A DUDE'S ATTENTION

LIKE, A LOT OF CHICKS ASK ME AND BEAVIS FOR ADVICE ABOUT DUDES, HUH HUH. THEY ALL WANT TO KNOW HOW TO GET A DUDE'S ATTENTION. OR AT ATTENTION, HUH HUH. I ALWAYS TELL CHICKS THE SAME THREE THINGS:

* TAKE OFF YOUR SHIRT, HUH HUH.
* UH, PLEASE TAKE OFF YOUR SHIRT.
* DAMMIT, I SAID PLEASE. GET BACK HERE AND LIKE, TAKE THAT THING OFF. OKAY, JUST UNBUTTON IT A LITTLE. THE TOP BUTTON. HUH HUH. OK, BYE NOW.

WHAT A DUDE SAYS AND WHAT HE REALLY MEANS

UM, HEH HEH. LIKE, HI. HEH HEH. UM, LET'S LIKE, LET'S GO SOMEWHERE AND UM DO IT. HEH HEH HEH. YEAH. NICE THINGIES.

TV IS COOL. LIKE, THEY SHOULD MAKE GLASSES THAT HAVE LIKE TWO TVS ON THE INSIDE SO YOU COULD LIKE PUT ON YOUR GLASSES AND YOU'D JUST BE WATCHING TV. HEH HEH. YOU'D BE ON YOUR BIKE WATCHING TV. I WONDER WHAT MY BIKE IS DOING RIGHT NOW. SOMEBODY'S PROBABLY LIKE, RIDING IT. HEH HEH M HEH HEH. RIDING IT. RIDE! RIDE! RIDE! MY NEXT BIKE IS GONNA BE MADE OF NACHOS. AND LIKE, THEN I CAN RIDE AND EAT AND WATCH TV. HEY, WHERE'D THAT CHICK GO? SHE WAS HERE JUST, UM, LIKE, 20 MINUTES AGO.

SKULL

DEATH ROCK

Ee EXCUSES THAT, LIKE, WORK

UM, EXCUSES ARE LIKE THESE THINGS YOU USE TO GET OUT OF STUFF, HEH HEH. IT'S LIKE MONEY, EXCEPT THEY DON'T BUY NACHOS, THEY JUST BUY TIME. AND LIKE, YOU CAN'T WAIT FOR STEWART BEFORE SCHOOL AND TAKE HIS. NOT EVERYBODY USES EXCUSES, BUT THAT'S CAUSE MOST PEOPLE AREN'T LIKE AS UNTELLIGENT AS US. HEH HEH. HERE'S SOME EXCUSES WE USE TO LIKE GET OUT OF STUFF.

* UM, A DOG ATE IT. HEH HEH. THEN HE PUKED IT BACK UP AND LIKE, ATE IT AGAIN. HEH HEH. THEN, WHEN HE PUKED IT UP AGAIN, HE JUST LIKE, ROLLED IN IT, HUH HUH. IT WAS MESSED UP.

* UH, HUH HUH. I COULDN'T GET TO WORK ON TIME CAUSE MY NADS HURT. HUH HUH.

* THIS FAT DUDE GEORGE BET US THAT LIKE WE WOULDN'T SPANK OUR MONKEYS AND THEN HIM AND HIS FRIENDS WERE LIKE BETTING TOO. UM, THIS DUDE JERRY AND ELAINE, WHO'S A CHICK, AND THIS OTHER DUDE NAMED CREAMER OR SOMETHING. AND SO LIKE WE WEREN'T DOING IT, HUH HUH. BUT LIKE, CREAMER DID IT AND THEN LIKE, HUH HUH, SO DID THE OTHERS, INCLUDING THE CHICK, WHO'S LIKE, NOT EVEN SPOSED TO HAVE A MONKEY, BUT SHE DID IT ANYWAY. HUH HUH. AND LIKE, THAT'S WHY WE COULDN'T DO THE HOMEWORK CAUSE WE WERE TOO BUSY NOT SPANKING OUR MONKEYS. BUT THEN DURING THE COMMERCIAL, WE DID. HUH HUH.

* UM, WE CAN'T LIKE PRECIPITATE IN THE CAN GOODS DRIVE CAUSE LIKE, WE'RE ALLERGENIC TO METAL, HEH HEH. UNLESS IT'S HEAVY.

* WE DIDN'T DO THE HOMEWORK CAUSE BEAVIS'S MOM HAD TO GO GET HER STOMACH PUMPED.

* UM, HEH HEH, WE DIDN'T DO THE ASSIGNMENT CAUSE WE WERE WATCHING EDUCATIONAL TV INSTEAD. YOU KNOW, LIKE A SHOW ABOUT THOSE THINGS, UM, DINOSSERS, HEH HEH. THEY WERE THOSE PURPLE THINGS WITH TEETH AND THEY LIKE, HUNG OUT WITH THE LITTLE CHILDREN AND SANG SONGS ABOUT NUMBERS AND CRAP. AND THEN THEY WENT SUXTINCT UNTIL A LITTLE LATER WHEN BIG BIRD CAME ON. THEY SAID ON THE SHOW YOU COULD GET A CLASS CREDIT FOR WATCHING.

* MY PEN RAN OUT OF INK. CAUSE LIKE I USED UP ALL THE INK WRITING, UH, TO THOSE POOR KIDS IN CENTRAL INDIANA.

* THESE DUDES JUMPED US AND LIKE MADE US GIVE THEM OUR HOMEWORK AND UM THEN THEY WENT TO THEIR SCHOOL AND LIKE, CLAIMED IT WAS THEIR HOMEWORK EVEN THOUGH IT WAS OURS. I HEARD THEY GOT A A ON IT. DON'T TRY TO FIND THEM CAUSE THEY LIVE IN ENGLAND OR LIKE BRITAIN OR SOMETHING.

* I HAVE THAT THING. UH, ATTENTION DEFI... UH, DEFI... HUH HUH HUH, DEFECATE. HUH HUH HUH HUH HUH.

* UH, WE'RE LATE FOR WORK CAUSE LIKE, WE WERE OUT FISHING WITH THE PRESIDENT OF BURGER WORLD. UH, HE SAID IT WAS OKAY SINCE HE'S THE PRESIDENT, AND ALSO THAT YOU HAVE TO LIKE CLEAN THE FRYER FOR US. HE SAID HE WAS PROBLY GONNA FIRE YOU UNLESS YOU LIKE GIVE US SOME MORE VACATIONS. HUH HUH.

Ff FOREINURZ

FRENCH DUDES

FRENCH DUDES LIKE TO SAY "OOH" A LOT. LIKE, "OOOH-LA-LA! VOOLEY VOO TAKE A LOOK AT THE POOH ON MY SHOE?" HEH HEH HEH.

FRENCH DUDES GET A LOT OF CHICKS, CAUSE THEY KNOW HOW TO FRENCH KISS, AND STUFF. PLUS THEY'VE GOT SOME, LIKE, MAGICAL WAY OF TICKLING. THIS WOULD BE OKAY IF THEY JUST GOT A LOT OF FRENCH CHICKS, BUT SOMETIMES THEY GET AMERICAN CHICKS TOO, WHICH SUCKS CAUSE THEN THERE'S LESS CHICKS FOR ME AND BEAVIS.

OH YEAH, AND FRENCH DUDES ALL THINK THAT SHARI LEWIS CHICK IS A GENIUS JUST CAUSE SHE, LIKE, TAUGHT A GOAT TO TALK.

CHINESE DUDES

YOU DON'T WANNA FIGHT CHINESE DUDES CAUSE THEY'RE ALL, LIKE, GOOD AT TAI-DYE AND STUFF, WHICH THEY LEARNED A LONG TIME AGO FROM THAT MARC POLIO DUDE.

PLUS THEY'VE HAD A LOT OF PRACTICE FIGHTING GODZILLA.

ANOTHER COOL THING ABOUT CHINESE DUDES IS THAT THEY CALL EVERYONE THEY MEET AN "AH-SO", HUH HUH HUH.

ENGLISH DUDES

ENGLISH DUDES ARE LIKE ENGLISH, BUT THE WEIRD THING IS, THEY DON'T TALK ENGLISH.

YEAH, HEH HEH. IT'S LIKE, WHEN THEY SAY "BUM" THEY'RE NOT TALKING ABOUT SOME DUDE BEGGING ON THE STREET, THEY'RE JUST TALKING ABOUT HIS BUTT.

HUH HUH. AND THEY SAY OTHER WEIRD STUFF LIKE, "IT'S TIME FOR TEA AND SPANK MY MONKEY."

YEAH, REALLY. ENGLISH DUDES ARE WAY TOO INTERESTED IN TEA.

MEXICAN DUDES

MEXICAN DUDES LOVE AMERICA ALMOST AS MUCH AS AMERICANS DO. LIKE, THEY NAMED THEIR WHOLE COUNTRY "SOUTH AMERICA" CAUSE THEY LOVE AMERICA SO MUCH. MAYBE THEY WERE HOPING WE'D RETURN THE FAVOR, AND THEN THE MOST ASS-KICKING COUNTRY IN THE WORLD WOULD BE CALLED "NORTH MEXICO." BUT INSTEAD WE JUST NAMED ONE STATE "NEW MEXICO." IT'S LIKE A CARNATION PRIZE OR SOMETHING.

THE ONLY WORDS THEY HAVE IN MEXICAN ARE, LIKE, FOODS: "NACHOS, TACOS, BURRITOS, TOSTADAS, CHIHUAHUAS AND CHIMICHANGAS."

YEAH BUT, UM, SOME OTHER MEXICAN FOOD ACKSHULLY HAS ENGLISH NAMES, LIKE RICE, BEANS, BURRITOS AND NACHOS.

WAIT. WAIT. UM, OH YEAH.

CANADIAN DUDES

JUST KEEP WALKING NORTH FOR ABOUT A MILLION MILES AND YOU'RE BOUND TO RUN INTO SOME CANADIAN DUDES. THEY'LL BE THE PEOPLE IN THE HOUSES MADE OUT OF ICE WHO SPEND ALL THEIR TIME HARPOONING WHALES. IT'S PROBLY A PRETTY COOL LIFE, BUT THE COLD WEATHER MUST REALLY, YOU KNOW, SHRIVEL YOUR THINGIE. LIKE YOU'D NOTICE WITH BEAVIS, HUH HUH.

SHUT UP, BUNGHOLE. CANADIAN DUDES HAVE, LIKE, A HUNDRED DIFFERENT WORDS FOR YELLOW SNOW.

DUTCH DUDES

NOT MUCH IS KNOWN ABOUT DUTCH DUDES, EXCEPT FOR THIS ONE KID WHO GOT HIS PICTURE ON ALL THE PAINT CANS AFTER HE PUT HIS FINGER IN A DYKE.

HEH HEH M HEH HEH. "CANS."

Ff THE FUTURE

IT'S IMPORTANT FOR A GOOD ENSUCKLOPEDIA TO HAVE STUFF ABOUT THE FUTURE. UH, BECAUSE KIDS IN THE FUTURE CAN STILL USE THIS BOOK TO CHEAT OFF OF. SO WE DID THAT THING. RESEARCH. LIKE WE WATCHED, THAT SHOW ABOUT THE, UM, DUDES IN THE SPACE SHIP AND THEY LIKE FLY TO DIFFERENT PLANETS OR WHATEVER AND THEY GET PHASERED ALL THE TIME. I THINK IT'S CALLED CHEERS. IT SUCKS. AND, UH, IN THE FUTURE, IT WILL STILL SUCK. HERE'S SOME OTHER STUFF.

LIFESTYLE

PROBLY THE BIGGEST QUESTION FOR ANY WUSS WHO GIVES A CRAP ABOUT THE FUTURE IS LIKE, WILL THEY FIND A WAY TO MAKE TV NOT SUCK? AND THE ANSWER IS NO, TV WILL NOT NOT SUCK, AND SINCE TWO WRONGS LIKE NUTRISIZE EACH OTHER, THAT MEANS TV WILL STILL SUCK. BUT THERE WILL BE SOME COOL THINGS. LIKE YOU'LL GO, "THIS SUCKS, CHANGE IT," AND LIKE, THE TV WILL AUTOMATICALLY FIND YOU SOME CHICKS AND EXPLOSIONS.

ALSO FOOD WILL BE DIFFERENT. BUT LIKE, IF THEY WANTED SOME REAL PROGRESS WITH FOOD, THEY SHOULD MAKE NACHOS THAT COME ALREADY CHEWED, OR LIKE INVENT HOT DOGS THAT COME IN THE FLAVORS OF FRUITY WHIPS SO IT'S LIKE, WHOA, A WHOLE MEAL IN A ROLL, THIS MUST BE THE FUTURE.

THERE'LL BE A LOT OF TECHNOLOGY CRAP TOO. WHEN YOU CALL SOMEBODY UP ON THE PHONE, FOR INSTANT, THEY'LL BE ON THIS LITTLE TV ON YOUR PHONE, SO IN THE FUTURE, PEOPLE WILL TRY TO CALL WHEN PEOPLE ARE IN THE SHOWER, OR, HUH HUH, DOING IT.

PEOPLE'LL COME FROM MILES AROUND TO WATCH THESE LIKE HUMAN AIR HOCKEY GAMES. IT'LL BE COOL.

LIKE, IF YOU SEE A TV WITH A SHARP POINT ON IT, IT'S PROBLY FROM THE FUTURE. IN THE FUTURE, TVS WILL BE EXTRA BIG LIKE THIS SO THEY CAN FIT MORE SHOWS INSIDE.

LIKE, IN THE FUTURE, YOU'LL BE ABLE TO CALL UP PEOPLE ON TV. YOU'LL GO UM, HELLO, BLOSSOM? YOUR SHOW SUCKS, HEH HEH HEH. THEN YOU CAN HANG UP AND LIKE, CALL THAT CHICK RHODA OR THAT ONE DUDE. HOGAN HERO.

TRAVEL

IN THE PAST, DUDES WENT SLOW. THEY RODE ON COWS OR SOMETHING, WHICH THEY HAD TO START BY SAYING, "GET UP." THEN THEY SAID, "THIS SUCKS. WE GOTTA GO FASTER! FASTER! FASTER!" THEN THAT DUDE CHEVY CHASE INVENTED THE CAR. BUT IT'S STILL NOT AS COOL AS IT COULD BE, CAUSE LIKE, A LOT OF CARS STILL DON'T PEEL OUT. BUT IN THE FUTURE, WHEN THEY'RE POWERED BY, LIKE, TECHNOLOGY OR SOMETHING, ALL CARS WILL FINALLY HAUL ASS. SO THERE'LL BE LIKE SKID MARKS AND GUYS RUNNING LIGHTS ALL OVER THE PLACE. THE FUTURE WILL BE COOL FOR ITS OUTSTANDING CRACKUPS.

THE FUTURE ALSO LIKE HAPPENS IN SPACE. THEY'LL HAVE THESE ROCKETS WITH THE POWER OF, LIKE, A THOUSAND M-80S, AND THEY GO TO OTHER PLANETS, LIKE, UH, MILKY WAY OR SNICKERS OR WHATEVER IT IS. AND WE'LL LIKE CIVILIZE IT WITH BURGER WORLDS AND HIGHWAYS AND STUFF. BUT, LIKE, NO SCHOOLS CAUSE WE DON'T WANT THOSE ILLEGAL ALIENS UP THERE LEARNING HOW TO KICK OUR ASS. THEN ME AND BEAVIS WILL MOVE TO ONE OF THOSE PLANETS TO LIKE COLONY IT AND NOT HAVE TO GO TO SCHOOL. HUH HUH HUH. WE'RE PRETTY SMART.

BUT THE COOLEST THING WILL BE THAT PEOPLE WILL HAVE THESE JETSON THINGS. THEY'RE LIKE BACKPACKS, ONLY THIS STUFF SHOOTS OUT THE BACK AND YOU CAN GO UP IN THE AIR, LIKE A BIRD, HUH HUH, AND DO STUFF LIKE BIRDS DO, LIKE PINCH LOAFS ON PEOPLE. IT'S PRETTY COOL, HUH HUH HUH. BUT LIKE, BY THEN THEY'LL HAVE LIKE A INVENTION OR SOMETHING THAT LIKE SHOOTS A LASER FROM YOUR HEAD TO A BIRD'S BUTT WHEN IT CRAPS ON YOU. HUH HUH. SO PINCHING LOAFS ON SOMEBODY'S HEAD WON'T BE AS COOL THEN AS IT IS NOW.

NOT EVERYTHING IN THE FUTURE WILL BE COOL. THERE'S STILL GONNA BE WUSSES LIKE THIS WITH BOOKS AND THINGS IN THEIR BACKPACKS. DUMBASS.

ECONOMICS

ONE OF THE BIG THINGS ABOUT ECOLOGICS IN THE FUTURE WILL BE ROBOTS. ROBOTS ARE THESE THINGS THAT'LL DO THE WORK HUMANS DON'T WANT TO DO, LIKE PICK UP AFTER YOU FOR THE HUNDREDTH TIME. THE COOL THING ABOUT ROBOTS IS, WE WON'T HAVE TO DEAL WITH A LOT OF BUTTMUNCH CUSTOMERS AT BURGER WORLD ANYMORE, CAUSE THEY'LL JUST LIKE SEND THEIR ROBOTS TO PICK UP THE FOOD FROM US. UH, WOULD YOU LIKE FRIES WITH THAT, YOU STUPID METAL FARTKNOCKER? HUH HUH HUH HUH.

JUST LIKE NOW, SOME JOBS WILL BE COOLER THAN OTHERS IN THE FUTURE. COOL JOBS WILL BE HOVERCRAFT REPAIRMAN, WORKING ON LIKE A VIDEO SEX PHONE, AND BEING OZZY. MOST OTHER JOBS WILL STILL SUCK.

CHICKS

CHICKS WILL BE DIFFERENT IN THE FUTURE. THEY'LL, LIKE, PUT OUT. CAUSE, UH, THEY'LL BE SMARTER, SO THEY'LL DIG US MORE. PLUS WE'LL BE LIKE OLDER, AND LEARNED WHATEVER IT IS OLD DUDES LEARN TO LIKE, MESMERIZE CHICKS. AND EVEN IF THIS PART OF THE FUTURE DOESN'T WORK OUT EXACTLY RIGHT, WE CAN PROBLY GET THOSE DUDES WHO MAKE ROBOTS TO MAKE US A ROBOT CHICK TO DO THE WORK HUMAN CHICKS WON'T DO. HUH HUH HUH HUH. THE FUTURE IS COOL.

POOR DUDES WILL HAVE AUTO-CHICKS LIKE THIS. AND IF YOU'RE LIKE RICH, YOU CAN GET ONE WITH A TV IN HER STOMACH.

THIS IS AN OLD PICTURE. LIKE, NOW WE KNOW IN THE REAL FUTURE, ROBOTS'LL BRING NACHOS.

Gg FEELING GOOD PAGE

WHEN YOU'RE SITTING AROUND, AND THINKING THAT LIFE SUCKS, YOU'RE PROBABLY RIGHT. BUT USUALLY THERE'S SOMETHING YOU CAN DO TO MAKE YOURSELF FEEL BETTER, HEH HEH. UNLESS YOU JUST DID IT, HEH HEH. THEN YOU CAN THINK ABOUT STUFF THAT MAKES YOU HAPPY. HERE'S LIKE A LIST.

TURDS. LIKE, WHAT IF THERE WERE NO TURDS? THERE'D BE LESS TOILETS.
OR MAYBE NOT, BUT IT'S STILL LIKE A COOL SUBJECT. TURDS.

WHEN IT'S LIKE A NICE DAY OUT, LIKE ON A SATURDAY, AND YOU WAKE UP AND GO, HM,
IT'S A NICE DAY, IT'S LIKE SUNNY AND STUFF. MAYBE THERE'LL BE SOMETHING GOOD ON TV.

ACCIDENTALLY RUNNING OVER SOMETHING ON YOUR BIKE.
THEN BACKING UP AND RUNNING OVER IT ON PURPOSE.

IT'S GOOD TO BE IN AMERICA CAUSE LIKE, ALL THE SIGNS AND STUFF
ARE IN A LANGUAGE YOU UNDERSTAND.

HOT CHICKS WHO HAVEN'T HAD THEIR BOYFRIENDS KICK YOUR ASS YET.

ONE TIME I WAS RUNNING BAREFOOT IN THIS VACANT LOT AND I CUT MY FOOT REALLY BAD.
AND I WAS ALWAYS BUMMED ABOUT IT UNTIL ONE DAY I THOUGHT, WHOA,
IF I'DA BEEN CRAWLING NAKED ON MY STOMACH IN THAT VACANT LOT,
IT COULDA CUT MY WEINER.

LITTLE KIDS ARE KINDA COOL. WHEN THEY LET YOU HANG OUT WITH THEM.

LOOK REAL CLOSE AT A FLOWER. THINK ABOUT HOW LONG IT TOOK THE FLOWER
TO GROW ALL ITS FLOWER CRAP. IT'S KIND OF INSTRESTING, SPECIALLY CAUSE IT
ONLY TAKES LIKE A MINUTE TO RIP IT APART.

SOMEWHERE, OUT AT A NACHO FARM OR LIKE A CHEESE FACTORY,
THERE'S LIKE A SNACK FOR ME THAT HASN'T EVEN BEEN MADE YET.
THEY BETTER HURRY UP, CAUSE I'M GETTING LIKE HUNGRY.

IF YOU'RE PISSED CAUSE ALL YOU DO IS LIKE SIT AROUND AND WATCH TV
ALL THE TIME, JUST GO LIKE, WELL, IT'S BETTER THAN SITTING
AROUND AND NOT WATCHING ANYTHING.

NADS ARE PRETTY COOL.

HARD - (SEE BEAVIS)

HEAD, CHICKEN - WHAT A CHICKEN RUNS AROUND WITHOUT FOR A FEW MINUTES AFTER YOU'VE CUT IT OFF. ITS HEAD, I MEAN. ALSO, LIKE, IF YOU GET THE RIGHT TRAINING AND LIKE KNOW SOMEBODY, YOU CAN GET A JOB AT THE SIDESHOW BITING THEM OFF. SOME DUDES HAVE ALL THE LUCK.

HEAD HUNTERS - THESE DUDES THAT, LIKE, GO UP TO CHICKS AND ASK THEM FOR, YOU KNOW, SOME OTHER DUDE'S HEAD ON A PLATE. UM, NOT TO BE CONFUSED WITH DUDES THAT HAVE PLATES IN THEIR HEADS, HEH HEH HEH!

HERTZ, ROD - UH, JUST ASK BEAVIS. HUH HUH HUH HUH HUH.

HOLIDAY - A DAY OFF WHEN YOU DON'T HAFTA GO TO SCHOOL OR WORK OR DO ANYTHING THAT SUCKS, CAUSE IT'S A DAY OFF. SOME HOLIDAYS ARE COOLER THAN OTHERS. LIKE, FOR ONE DAY EVERY OCTOBER THERE'S A "JULY FOURTH" HOLIDAY CELEBRATING WHEN WE OFFISHULLY TOLD ENGLAND THAT WE WERE GOING TO KICK ITS ASS. THAT'S PRETTY COOL! BUT THEN THERE'S, LIKE, "PRESIDENTS' DAY" WHICH CELEBRATES TWO PRESIDENTS' BIRTHDAYS, BUT YOU ONLY GET ONE DAY OFF CAUSE THEY WERE, LIKE, TWINS. OR MAYBE THEY WEREN'T TWINS, BUT THEIR PARENTS JUST DECIDED TO CELEBRATE THEIR BIRTHDAYS ON THE SAME DAY TO SAVE MONEY ON PRESENTS AND STUFF. PRESIDENTS' DAY SUCKS!

HORMONE - HOW DO YOU MAKE A HORMONE? UH, WHAT DO I LOOK LIKE, THAT SNOOP DOGGY HAUSER DUDE?

INDIAN BURN - KINDA LIKE, WHEN YOU SPANK SOME DUDE'S ARM FOR HIM? IT GOT ITS NAME CAUSE THIS IS HOW INDIANS WOULD START CAMP-FIRES, BY RUBBING TWO DUDES' ARMS TOGETHER.

THEY DID THIS SO OFTEN THEY, LIKE, WOUNDED THEIR KNEES, OR SOMETHING.

INFORMATION SUPERHIGHWAY - UH, IT'S LIKE THIS, UH, SUPERHIGHWAY FULL OF, YOU KNOW, INFORMATION? LIKE IN THE ADS: "HAVE YOU EVER HAD A MEETING IN YOUR BARE BUTT? WELL, YOU WILL, AND THE COMPANY THAT'LL BRING IT TO YOU IS T&A, OR SOMETHING." HUH HUH HUH! NO WAY, BUTT-HEAD! THE INFORNICATION SUPERHIGHWAY IS, LIKE, WHERE DEATH TRUCK FIGURES OUT WHO TO KILL NEXT.

INSECT - EH HEH HEH, IF YOU REALLY WANNA KNOW WHAT AN INSECT IS, JUST SCRATCH YOUR BUTT OR YOUR NADS OR SOMETHING AND THEN CHECK UNDER YOUR NAILS. ANYTHING YOU SEE THAT'S STILL MOVING IS PROBLY AN INSECT.

INTELLIGENCE - THAT'S THIS THING IN YOUR HEAD THAT'S LIKE GAS IN A TANK. SOMEBODY PUT SUGAR IN BEAVIS'S, HUH HUH. SHUT UP, BUTTWIPE. SERIOUSLY, THOUGH, LIKE YOU CAN FILL UP AN EMPTY GAS TANK, BUT IF YOU'RE NATURALLY UNINTELLIGENT, THERE'S LIKE NO WAY YOU CAN GET GAS FOR YOUR HEAD, OR SOMETHING. THEY SAY SCHOOL HELPS, BUT THEY'RE JUST TRYING TO SEE IF YOU'RE DUMB ENOUGH TO FALL FOR IT.

INTERCOURSE, HAVE SEKSUAL - (SEE IT, DO)

IT, DO - UH, YOU KNOW, THAT'S LIKE WHEN YOU AND A CHICK, LIKE, HAVE SEKSUAL INTERCOURSE? OH YEAH, AND IT'S ALSO "A CONJOINING OF THE MALE AND FEMALE GENITALS FOR THE PURPOSES OF PROCREATION" OR SOMETHING. I'M NOT SURE WHAT THAT SECOND THING MEANS, BUT THAT'S WHAT IT SAID IN THIS BIG DICTIONARY IN THE LIBRARY AT SCHOOL. HUH HUH, I WROTE "BIG DICTIONARY!"

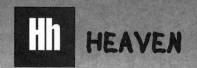
HEAVEN

WHEN HE JUDGES YOUR LIFE, GOD DOESN'T LOOK AT COOL STUFF YOU DID LIKE KICKING GUY'S ASSES AND STUFF. IT'S LIKE YOU HAVE TO DO DIFFERENT STUFF FOR GOD TO THINK YOU'RE COOL. LIKE, YOU HAVE TO PASS HIS INITIATION RITUALS, LIKE CHURCH. AND THEN YOU GET TO GO TO HIS CLUBHOUSE, WHICH IS LIKE HEAVEN. AND THIS IS WHAT'S IN IT.

CLOUDS – HEAVEN IS LIKE BUILT OF CLOUDS. SO LIKE, WHEN YOU SEE A LOT OF CLOUDS IN THE SKY, IT MEANS THAT SOMEBODY IS LIKE STEALING CONSTRUCTION MATERIALS FROM LIKE A NEW DEVELOPMENT IN HEAVEN.

ST. PETER – ST. PETER HAS A BIG BOOK THAT HAS EVERYTHING YOU DID IN IT. THAT'S LIKE A BIG DEAL IN HEAVEN, BOOKS AND STUFF. IT'S LIKE, THEY SHOULD CHANGE THAT EXPRESSO TO, "IT'S LIKE I DIED AND WENT TO COLLEGE, OR SOMETHING." ALSO, DON'T MAKE FUN OF PETER'S NAME, OR HE'LL PUT LIGHTNING UP YOUR BUTT.

ANGELS – ALL THE PEOPLE WHO WORSHIPPED GOD ON EARTH AND LIKE MEANT IT GET TO BE ANGELS. THAT MEANS THEY GET TO FLY AROUND AND PLAY OLD TIME GUITARS AND STUFF. BUT WHAT SUCKS IS THAT ONLY GOD AND JESUS AND HIS LIKE ROADIES GET TO HAVE BEARDS AND STUFF. IT'S LIKE ZZ TOP'S FAMILY OR SOMETHING.

"NO CHICKS" SIGN – IT USED TO BE IN OLDEN TIMES THAT THEY WOULDN'T LET CHICKS INTO HEAVEN. THEN THEY CHANGED THE RULE IN THE 60S, BUT THEY STILL SAID, "THOU SHALT NOT, LIKE, DO IT." BUT PROBABLY PEOPLE SNEAK OFF AND DO IT ANYWAY.

PEARLY GATES – HEAVEN IS FAMOUS FOR ITS PEARLY GATES, WHICH WERE, UH, BUILT IN 1914 AT A COST OF 20 THOUSAND DOLLARS. HUH HUH. THEY'RE PROBABLY

ALSO LECTRIFIED, BUT NOBODY REALLY KNOWS. SOME SAY YES, SOME SAY NO.

GOD'S THRONE — GOD SITS ON THIS BIG THRONE AND LIKE TIMIDATES PEOPLE INTO BEING WUSSES. BUT HE DOESN'T SIT ON IT ALL THE TIME. IT'S LIKE WHEN SANTA'S IN THE MALL. SOMETIMES HE HAS TO GO AND LIKE SIT ON THE OTHER THRONE, HUH HUH. HE'S GOT A SIGN THAT GOES, "GOD WILL BE BACK AT 1:30."

LOST PLANES — SOMETIMES, WHEN PLANES DISAPPEAR OVER THE BERMUDA TRIANGLE, THEY WIND UP IN HEAVEN, AND THEY HAVE TO LIKE CIRCLE AROUND UNTIL ALL THE PASSENGERS DIE OF NATURAL CAUSES. THEN THEY GET TAKEN INTO HEAVEN OR WHATEVER, AND GOD USES THE PLANES FOR HIS AIR FORCE.

TVs — THEY HAVE LIKE BIG SCREEN TVs IN HEAVEN, AND YOU CAN WATCH LIKE ANYONE'S LIFE YOU WANT. IT'S LIKE, YOU CAN SAY, "STEWART'S LIFE SUCKS, CHANGE IT," AND YOU CAN WATCH PEOPLE LIKE DOING IT, HUH HUH. BUT THEN THEY BLOCK THE TVs FROM LIKE SHOWING THE GOOD PARTS.

PETTING ZOO — HEAVEN HAS LIKE A COOL PETTING ZOO. LIKE, ALL THE ANIMALS ARE LIKE REALLY FURRY AND SOFT AND YOU CAN LIKE FEED THEM SANDWICHES AND LIKE SMALLER ANIMALS AND STUFF AND THEY LIKE IT— UH, BEAVIS. SHUT UP.

WANTED POSTERS — EVERYBODY'S SUCH A WUSS IN HEAVEN THAT WHEN WE GET THERE, WE'LL PROBABLY BE ABLE TO KICK PEOPLE IN THE NADS AND RIP OFF CANDY AND STUFF FOR A COUPLE YEARS BEFORE THEY FINALLY PUT A REWARD ON US. THEN WE'LL GO HIDE OUT IN HELL FOR A WHILE, AND JUST GO UP TO HEAVEN WHEN WE NEED SOME CLOUDS OR SOMETHING.

GOD
WILL BE
BACK AT
1:30

WANTED

NO CHICKS

THOR, THE NORTH GOD OF THUNDER

A LONG TIME AGO THERE WERE THESE, LIKE, NORTHMEN OR WHATEVER WHO WERE REALLY STUPID. WHENEVER THEY HEARD THUNDER, THEY DIDN'T KNOW IT WAS CAUSED BY WEATHER STUFF. THEY THOUGHT IT WAS CAUSED BY SOME BUTTMUNCH NAMED THOR WHO LIVED IN THE SKY. HUH HUH. DORKS. THEY THOUGHT WHENEVER SOMEONE PULLED HIS FINGER, HE WOULD FART LIGHTNING. SOMETIMES IN A REALLY BAD STORM, HE WOULD FART SO MUCH HE WOULD PRACTICALLY TEAR HIMSELF A NEW CORNHOLIO. THAT'S WHY HE WAS CALLED THOR. HE WOULD GO AROUND AND SAY, "I'M THOR." AND PEOPLE WOULD SAY, "YEAH, WELL MAYBE YOU SHOULD GET YOURSELF A NEW *BUNGHOLE!*"

THE RIDDLE OF THE SPHINCTER

IN ANCIENT EGYPT THERE WAS THIS THING CALLED THE SPHINCTER THAT HAD THE HEAD OF A MAN AND THE BODY OF LIKE A DOG. HE WAS REAL WISE AND ALSO HE COULD LICK HIS NADS WHENEVER HE WANTED. ALSO HE WAS LIKE 200 FEET TALL, AND HE HAD THIS RIDDLE THAT IF YOU GUESSED IT RIGHT YOU GOT TO DO IT WITH HIS DAUGHTER WHO HAD LIKE 50-FOOT BOOBS, BUT IF YOU GUESSED IT WRONG YOU GOT KILLED. SO, LIKE, EITHER WAY YOUR FRIENDS HAD SOMETHING TO WATCH.

ONE DAY SOME EGYPTIAN DUDE WHO HAD A STIFFY TO SEE THE BOOBS TRIED TO ANSWER THE RIDDLE. THE SPHINCTER SAID, "WHAT HAS FOUR LEGS IN THE MORNING, THREE LEGS AT NOON AND --" NO WAIT, UH -- "WHAT HAS THREE LEGS IN THE MORNING --"

UH, HUH HUH -- "THE ANSWER IS BEAVIS."
SHUT UP, DILLHOLE!
ANYWAY THE SPHINCTER ASKED HIM THIS REALLY HARD RIDDLE WHICH THE EGYPTIAN GUY DIDN'T KNOW, AND SO HE PLEADED WITH THE SPHINCTER, "OH MIGHTY SPHINCTER, PLEASE DON'T KILL ME, I DON'T NEED TO SEE THE BOOBS." SO THE SPHINCTER SAID, "PULL MY FINGER." AND WHEN THE GUY DID, THE SPHINCTER'S 20-FOOT NOSE FELL OFF AND CRUSHED HIM.
AND ALL THROUGHOUT EGYPT-LAND, PEOPLE THOUGHT THAT WAS COOL. AND THEY BOWED DOWN AND WORSHIPED THE SPHINCTER. AND THEY NAMED A PART OF THEIR BUTT AFTER HIM.

MOTOR LISA, BEFORE AND AFTER
LEONARDO DA FONZI WAS A FAMOUS FOREN GUY WHO TOLD CHICKS HE WAS A PAINTER SO THEY WOULD TAKE OFF THEIR CLOTHES AND GET NAKED. THEN HE'D GO TO THE BATHROOM, AND THE CHICKS WOULD SAY, "HEY LEONARDO, WHAT'RE YOU DOING IN THERE?" AND HE'D SAY, "I'M STRETCHING MY CANVAS," OR, "I'M PRACTICING MY STROKES," OR, "I'M SQUEEZ-ING PAINT FROM MY TUBE." HUH HUH.

DA FONZI HAD THE HOTS FOR THIS STUCK-UP BIKER CHICK NAMED MOTOR LISA WHO HAD REALLY BIG HOOTERS. BUT SHE WOULDN'T LET HIM SEE THEM, EVEN THOUGH HE BEGGED HER. HE SAID, "I AM AN *ARTEEST*. I WANT TO, LIKE, PAINT ZE NIPPLES OR SOMETHING. AND THEN WE CAN, YOU KNOW, DO EET." BUT MOTOR LISA GOT ALL HUFFY AND SAID, "I AM SAVING MY HOOTERS FOR THE MAN I MARRY," AND THAT KIND OF CRAP.
DA FONZI DECIDED TO LOOSEN HER UP. HE ASKED MOTOR LISA TO PULL HIS FINGER. THE SOUND OF HIS FART MADE HER SMILE. HE PAINTED HER SMILING. THEN HE PAINTED HER AS SHE GOT A WHIFF OF THE FRUITS OF HIS MIGHTY FARTULENCE.

Ii THE DECLARATION OF INDEPENDENTS

HOW AMERICA TOLD THAT SUCKY COUNTRY BRITIN TO SHOVE IT UP THEIR BUTTHOLE.

* * * * * * *

LIKE ON THE FOURTH OF JULY, 1976, A BUNCH OF OLD DUDES WROTE THE DECLARATION OF INDEPENDENTS AND BLEW OFF A BUNCH OF FIREWORKS AND BOTTLE ROCKETS.

IT'S KINDA LIKE, BRITIN IS THIS LITTLE DINGLEBERRY OF A COUNTRY. SO THESE DUDES TOOK THIS PIECE OF PAPER AND JUST WIPED BRITIN, AND TOLD THEM TO GET OFF OUR BUTT.

Uhhh, four score (huh huh) and uh, a bunch of years ago, we the people, like, declare our independents or something. And the rockers red glare, the bombs bursting in air. Uhhh... like, most dudes are created equal (except Beavis) and have certain aliens rights. like, the right to bare chicks and the right to remain silent. Cause sometimes you gotta fight for your right to party. With liberty and Justice for all. Amen. Uhhh... thank you, Cleveland.

— John Hancock

Speech bubble: PULL BEAVIS'S FINGER

GET A SMALL CARDBOARD BOX AND CUT A HOLE IN THE BOTTOM. THEN TAKE SOME, LIKE, STUFFING AND PUT IT IN THE BOX SO NOBODY CAN SEE THE HOLE. THEN GET SOME RED PAINT AND PAINT THE INSIDE OF THE BOX, SO IT LOOKS LIKE THERE'S BLOOD IN THERE. THEN CUT OFF ONE OF BEAVIS'S FINGERS AND PUT IT IN THE BOX.

NEXT TIME YOU'RE AT A SWIMMING POOL, JUST, LIKE, TAKE A LEAK IN IT. THE GOOD THING IS, YOU DON'T EVEN HAFTA TAKE YOUR BATHING SUIT OFF TO DO THIS.

Jj PRACTICUL JOKES

CALL UP, LIKE, A SPORTING GOODS STORE OR SOMETHING? AND ASK IF THEY HAVE LIKE, A CASE OF VOLLEY BALLS. HUH HUH HUH HUH. "BALLS!"

CALL SOMEONE UP AND ASK THEM IF PRINCE ALBERT IS STILL SITTING ON THE CAN.

BUILD YOUR OWN MONSTER, JUST LIKE THAT DR. FRANKENBERRY DUDE, AND THEN TURN IT LOOSE IN THE GIRLS' LOCKER ROOM. THEY'LL PROBABLY ALL COME RUNNING OUT WITH THEIR CLOTHES OFF.

CALL UP ONE OF THOSE PHONE SEX NUMBERS, HUH HUH, BUT MAKE IT A COLLECT CALL, SO YOU DON'T HAFTA PAY. THAT'D BE COOL!

M HEH HEH, HERE'S A REALLY FUNNY ONE: CALL A CHICK UP AND ASK HER IF SHE WANTS A DATE.

HUH HUH, YOU DUMBASS, BEAVIS. THAT'S NOT A PRACTICUL JOKE.

SHUT UP BUTT-HEAD. THEY ALWAYS LAUGH WHEN I DO IT.

NEXT TIME YOU'RE AT A CARNIVAL? GO IN THE HOUSE OF MIRRORS AND TAKE OUT YOUR WEINER.

BUY A WHOLE BUNCH OF BALLOONS. YOU KNOW, THE KIND THAT'S FILLED WITH HELIUM? AND TIE THEM ONTO YOUR SCHOOL. ONCE YOU GET ENOUGH BALLOONS, YOUR WHOLE SCHOOL WILL GO AWAY. I SAW TODD DO THAT ONCE. REALLY.

GO TO A NUDE BEACH.

CALL SOMEONE UP AND SAY YOU'RE FROM THE PHONE COMPANY, AND THAT YOU'RE GONNA, LIKE, TEST THEIR PHONE LINE. THEN DON'T TEST THEIR PHONE LINE.

DISGUISE YOURSELF AS ONE OF THOSE MONEY MACHINES THAT BANKS HAVE. WHEN SOME RICH DUDE COMES ALONG TO MAKE A DEPOSIT, YOU CAN JUST KEEP ALL HIS MONEY.

TELL SOME CHICK THAT YOU LOVE HER, SO SHE'LL DO IT WITH YOU. HUH HUH HUH. BUT DON'T FALL FOR THIS TRICK IF SOME CHICK SAYS SHE LOVES YOU.

Jj J IS FOR JOBS

THEY SAY THAT MONEY MAKES THE WORLD ROUND OR SOMETHING. BUT LIKE, YOU CAN'T SIT ON YOUR ASS AND EXPECT TO GET ENOUGH MONEY TO DO COOL STUFF LIKE HANG OUT. THAT'S WHERE, LIKE, JOBS COME IN.

THERE ARE LIKE TWO KINDS OF JOBS: ONE IS CALLED "JOBS," WHICH IS FOR JOBS THAT SUCK, AND THE OTHER KIND IS CALLED "CAREERS," WHICH ALSO SUCK, BUT FOR LONGER. HERE'S LIKE A FEW JOBS THAT PEOPLE DO, NOT INCLUDING GETTING US PISSED OFF, WHICH IS LIKE A JOB ALMOST EVERYONE HAS.

DOCTOR – THIS GUY OPERATES ON YOU AND GIVES YOU SHOTS AND STUFF. BUT IT'S NOT AS MUCH FUN AS IT SOUNDS, CAUSE LIKE YOU HAVE TO GO TO SCHOOL EXTRA FOR IT. ON THE OTHER HAND YOU ALSO GET TO SEE CHICKS NAKED, WHICH <u>IS</u> AS MUCH FUN AS IT SOUNDS, HUH HUH.

BUSINESSMAN – TO BE A BUSINESSMAN, YOU HAVE TO WEAR A TIE AND HARD SHOES AND SIT IN THESE THINGS. MEETINGS OR SOMETHING. IT'S LIKE CHURCH, EXCEPT IT LASTS ALL WEEK AND THE GUY IN CHARGE DOESN'T OFFER YOU NACHOS TO STAY FOR "CHOIR PRACTICE." BUT, LIKE, A LOT OF BUSINESS-MEN MUST WORK FOR THE CIA OR SOMETHING CAUSE NOBODY KNOWS WHAT WORK THEY REALLY DO. SOME PEOPLE SAY THEY DO NO WORK AT ALL, EXCEPT IT <u>IS</u> PRETTY HARD TO TIE A TIE.

LUMBERJACK – HUH HUH. JACK. THEY CUT DOWN TREES AND YELL SOMETHING, IT SOUNDS LIKE "TEN-FOUR" OR SOMETHING. THEN THEY LIKE TAKE THE LOGS AND TURN THEM INTO PENCILS AND MATCHES AND STUFF. WORKING WITH LOGS IS PRETTY COOL. JUST ASK BEAVIS.

FARMER – THESE GUYS GROW MILK AND TREES AND FOOD, AND THEY LIKE PLOW FIELDS, HUH HUH. THEN THEY LISTEN TO COUNTRY MUSIC AND WALK AROUND TELLING TRAVELING SALESMEN NOT TO DO IT WITH THEIR DAUGHTERS. IT'S PRETTY COOL, EXCEPT FOR THE COUNTRY MUSIC. AND PLUS, IT'S COOL TO HAVE LIKE A DAUGHTER, CAUSE IT MEANS YOU MUSTA DONE IT ONCE, EVEN IF IT WAS A LONG TIME AGO, HEH HEH HEH HEH. OR LIKE YOUR WIFE DID OR SOMETHING.

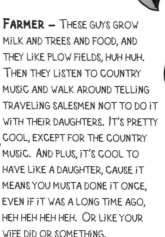

COLLEGE MUSICIAN – LIKE, THIS IS A COOL JOB, EXCEPT YOU GOTTA GO AROUND SAYING HOW EVERYTHING'S ALL MESSED UP AND STUFF, AND YOU'RE LIKE ALL PISSED OFF ABOUT IT. PLUS YOU HAVE TO PLAY SUCKY MUSIC, BUT IF YOU WENT TO COLLEGE, YOU PROBABLY GOT TAUGHT TO LIKE SUCKY MUSIC, SO IT'S NOT SO BAD. EXCEPT SUCKY MUSIC, UH, SUCKS, SO MAYBE IT IS. BAD. ANYWAY, ALL THE COOL MUSICIAN JOBS ARE GONNA BE TAKEN BY US, SO COLLEGE MUSICIAN IS ALL THAT'S GONNA BE OPEN.

SOLDIER – LIKE, WHEN YOU'RE IN THE ARMY, ALL THE CHICKS GO, "HEY, SAILOR!" AND YOU GET TO WEAR TATTOOS AND STAND AT ATTENTION, WHICH WE'RE LIKE ALREADY REALLY GOOD AT, HEH HEH. THE ARMY IS ALSO COOL CAUSE THEY CAN TEACH YOU HOW TO KILL A MAN WITH YOUR BARE HANDS, BUT IF YOU'RE LIKE A BAD STUDENT, THEY GIVE YOU A GUN.

COP – YOU GET TO BE ON TV AND SAY THINGS LIKE "WE BUSTED THE PERP," AND STUFF. AND, LIKE, YOU GET TO SAY, "YOU'LL HAVE A LOT OF TIME TO THINK ABOUT THAT WHERE YOU'RE GOING, PUNK." AND, LIKE, "ASSUME THE POSITION." HEH HEH. WHEN YOU SAY "ASSUME," YOU SAY A WORD THAT HAS "ASS" IN IT. IT DOESN'T GET MUCH COOLER THAN THAT.

GARBAGEMAN – LIKE, WHAT CAN YOU SAY ABOUT A JOB THAT LETS YOU RIDE ON A TRUCK AND THROW STUFF AROUND AT 5 IN THE MORNING AND GO THROUGH PEOPLE'S CRAP? UH, NOTHING. EXCEPT THAT IT'S PRETTY COOL. ALSO THIS IS A GOOD JOB TO HAVE IF YOU'RE GOING OUT WITH A CHICK, CAUSE YOU CAN GET HER PRESENTS AND STUFF FOR FREE.

CONSTRUCTION WORKER – THESE GUYS GET TATTOOS AND TAKE COFFEE BREAKS AND BUILD STUFF AND, HEH HEH, THEY LAY PIPE. AND IN A LOT OF JOBS, IF YOU'RE FAT IT SUCKS, BUT HERE A GUT IS LIKE A BADGE OF HONOR. IF YOU HAVE A TATTOO AND A GUT, YOU'RE LIKE A KING, OR SOME-THING. PLUS THEY ALSO KNOW HOW TO TALK TO CHICKS. LIKE, THEY DON'T TALK, THEY JUST WHISTLE. IT'S LIKE A LOVE SONG OR SOMETHING.

IMPORTANT THINGS

- IN THE DESERT, YOU CAN DO A LOT MORE STUFF WITHOUT GETTING CAUGHT BY THE COPS.
- IF YOU HAVE INSURANCE, YOU CAN CUT OFF YOUR ARM AND GET, LIKE, A MILLION DOLLARS.
- YOUR MOM MAY OWE YOU MONEY. SO YOU SHOULD GET A LAWYER. I, LIKE, SAW IT ON OPRAH.
- YOUR MOM MAY NOT BE YOUR MOM AFTER ALL.
- NEXT TIME YOU PICK UP A HANDFUL OF DIRT, JUST REMEMBER THAT IT MIGHT HAVE ONCE BEEN AN ANIMAL TURD.
- THE WATER IN THE TOILET MAKES YOUR TURDS LOOK BIGGER THAN THEY REALLY ARE.
- EATING MAKES YOU GO TO THE BATHROOM.
- YOU CAN STILL GET WOOD WHEN YOU'RE REALLY OLD.
- YOU DON'T GO BLIND FROM, YOU KNOW.

TO KNOW

- You can't run out of sperm from, you know.
- It's against the law to make a chick do it with you. That's why guys have to, you know, make friends with themselves.
- Jail dudes get to watch TV all day.
- Roosters wake people up in the morning. Roosters are sometimes called cocks. Huh huh. So don't be surprised if you get woken up by morning rooster. Huh huh huh.
- Sometimes bald dudes have hairy butts.
- Oprah says fat people can't help it.
- School counselors never tell you that instead of going to college, you can buy a car.
- A lot of chicks sleep naked. The really hot ones.

LI LITERATER

YOU KNOW THOSE THINGS? THEY GOT LIKE PAPER INSIDE AND YOU LIKE USE THEM FOR SMASHING BUGS AND STUFF, UNLESS THERE'S NOTHING TO SMASH AND SO YOU JUST LIKE READ EM OR WHATEVER? THOSE THINGS ARE CALLED BOOKS. THIS IS LIKE A LIST OF THE BEST BOOKS EVER WROTE.

MOBY DICK

UM, HEH HEH. WHAT'S BIG AND WHITE, HEH HEH. AND THERE'S LIKE, LOTS OF SAILORS ON IT, HEH HEH. HEH HEH HEH HEH HEH. UM, THE BOOK SUCKS, BUT LIKE, THE NAME OF IT MAKES UP FOR ALL THE SUCKY PARTS. I WOULDN'T UM RECOMMEND IT OR WHATEVER UNLESS YOU'RE JUST LOOKING FOR A BOOK WITH A GOOD NAME. STEWART SAYS THERE'S A DUDE WITH A WOODEN LEG IN IT, BUT, LIKE, BIG DEAL. I'VE GOT ONE OF THOSE MYSELF. HEH HEH. SEE IT? HEH HEH M HEH HEH.

NAKED BIKER MAGAZINE,

AUGUST 1993—UH, HUH HUH, THIS IS A MAGAZINE THAT WE GOT FOR FREE AT THE SWIF MART, HUH HUH HUH. IT'S MOSTLY ABOUT CHICKS WHO LIKE TO RIDE AROUND ON MOTORCYCLES NAKED. IT LIKE TEACHES YOU STUFF. LIKE STUFF ABOUT MOTORCYCLES AND CHICKS AND HOW THEY'RE LIKE PRETTY MUCH THE SAME. PLUS IT'S LIKE EASY TO HOLD WITH ONE HAND. HUH HUH HUH.

WHERE THE WILD THING IS

HUH HUH HUH. IN MY PANTS, HUH HUH.

CURRY GREG OR SOMETHING

UM, THIS IS THIS BOOK AND IT'S ABOUT THIS LITTLE MONKEY DUDE AND HE LIKE LIVES WITH THIS OTHER DUDE WITH A YELLOW HAT, HEH HEH HEH. YEAH, AND LIKE THE MONKEY IS UM REAL CURRY OR WHATEVER, SO HE LIKE GETS IN TROUBLE AND STUFF, HEH HEH, CAUSE HE LIKE MESSES WITH STUFF. AND THEN THE YELLOW HAT DUDE HAS TO GO SAVE THE MONKEY DUDE'S ASS. HEH HEH. HEY BEAVIS. DOES HE EVER SPANK THE MONKEY? HUH HUH HUH HUH HUH. HEH HEH HEH HEH. SHUT UP, BUTT-HEAD. HE'S NOT LIKE THAT. IT'S A GOOD BOOK. IT'S LIKE, INSTRESTING OR SOMETHING.

MATCHBOOK FROM THE CLASSY CAT LOUNGE

ONE TIME, VAN DRIESSEN MADE US WRITE A BOOK REPORT ABOUT ANY BOOK WE WANTED TO. AND, UM, LIKE, WE DID IT ON A BOOK OF MATCHES. HEH HEH HEH HEH. AND LIKE, HE HAD TO LET US DO IT, CAUSE HE SAID IT COULD BE ABOUT ANY BOOK WE WANTED. AND YOU KNOW WHAT? IT WAS A PRETTY GOOD BOOK. HEH HEH. VAN DRIESSEN STILL GAVE US A D, THOUGH. FARTKNOCKER.

DEATHSPAWN #396

THIS IS THE DEATHSPAWN ONE WHERE DEATHSPAWN KILLS THAT DUDE BY LIKE PUNCHING HIM IN THE HEAD AND PULLING OUT HIS BRAINS AND THEN SHOWING THEM TO THE DUDE BEFORE HE DIES. HUH HUH HUH. DEATHSPAWN RULES. IT'S LIKE, IF HE TOOK OUT BEAVIS'S BRAINS AND SHOWED THEM TO HIM, HE'D SEE LIKE CHICKS' THINGIES AND NACHOS AND SOME TOILETS AND LIKE A BUNCH OF CRAP LIKE THAT. HUH HUH.

SHUT UP, BUNGHOLE. HE WOULDN'T EVEN BE ABLE TO FIND YOUR BRAINS CAUSE THEY'RE LIKE IN YOUR BUTT, HEH HEH HEH.

BEAVIS, YOU'RE LIKE SICK OR SOMETHING. SERIOUSLY.

THE CATCHER IN THE RYE

THIS IS ABOUT THIS KID AND, UM, I THINK HIS NAME WAS CATCHER OR SOMETHING. HE, LIKE, SWEARS ALL THE TIME. THAT'S PRETTY COOL. PLUS HE CALLS PEOPLE PHONES, HEH HEH. LIKE, UM, THAT DUDE IS A BIG PHONE. AND HIS SISTER'S NAME IS PHONE TOO. HEH HEH. CATCHER'S LIKE STUPID AND MESSED UP, BUT HE'S COOL. HE'S KIND OF LIKE CURRY GREG, BUT NO HAT GUY.

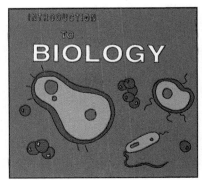

LORD OF THE RINGS

WHEN YOU SMASH A BUG WITH THIS BOOK, HUH HUH, THAT BUG STAYS, UH, LIKE SMASHED. HUH HUH. THIS BOOK IS COOL.

INTRODUCTION TO BIOLOGY

HUH HUH HUH. YOU KNOW HOW, LIKE, WHEN A DOG GETS HIT BY A CAR AND THERE'S LIKE ALL THE GUTS ALL OVER THE PLACE? THIS BOOK TELLS YOU LIKE THE NAMES OF ALL THE GUTS AND STUFF. HUH HUH. PLUS IT'S GOT LIKE A DRAWING OF TWO CHICKENS DOING IT. HUH HUH.

Mm UH, HUH HUH HUH HUH

ADJUSTING YOUR SET
BATTING PRACTICE
BEING YOUR OWN BEST FRIEND
CHANGING YOUR OIL
COOKING SOME SHEET MEAT
DISHONORABLE DISCHARGE
DOING SOME RAPID ONE-ARM PULL-UPS
EMPTYING THE PAYLOAD
FATHERING SOME PLEASURE
FIRING YOUR SQUIRT GUN
FIST-KEBABING
FREEING THE WILLIES
GETTING YOUR PALM RED
GOING BACK TO NATURE
GUNNING THE MOTOR
HITTING THE BATSMAN
HOMECOMING
HONING THE BONE
IRONING SOME WRINKLES
JUNIOR OLYMPIC POLE VAULTING
KNUCKLING YOUR KNOB
LAUNCHING THE HAND SHUTTLE
LECTRIFYING THE CATTLE PROD
LETTING SOME AIR OUT OF YOUR TIRE
MANNING THE COCKPIT
MASHING THE MONSTER
MEASURING FOR CONDOMS
MILKING YOUR BANANA
PEELING THE CARROT
PLAYING HAND HOCKEY

PLAYING THE PIPE ORGAN
PUD WRESTLING
PUNCHING YOUR WAY INTO HEAVEN
ROASTING YOUR WEINER
ROLLING YOUR JAM JOINT
ROUGHING UP THE SUSPECT
SELF-WHITTLING
SENDING OUT THE TROOPS
SHAKING THE THERMOMETER
SHIFTING GEARS
SHOOTING SOME SEEDS
SNAKE CHARMING
SOLOING
SPEAR FISHING
SPEED KNEADING
SPREADING THE MAYO
SQUEEZING OUT THE TOOTHPASTE
STAFF MEETING
TAKING A SHAKE BREAK
TAMING YOUR SNAKE
THREADING THE NEEDLE
THROTTLE THE BOTTLE
TOSSING THE JAVELIN
TUGGING YOUR TAPIOCA TUBE
TUNING THE ANTENNA
VIRTUAL SEX
VISITING MR. O.
WALKING THE LOG
WEDDING REHEARSAL
WHITEWATER WRISTING

history of

HEAVY METAL KICKS ASS. IT'S AN ART FARM OR SOMETHING. YOU SHOULD, LIKE, CRANK IT IN THE MORNING, CAUSE IT'S BETTER THAN THAT COFFEE CRAP, AND IT TAKES YOUR MIND OFF STUFF THAT SUCKS. PLUS IF YOU CRANK IT LOUD ENOUGH, YOUR NEIGHBORS WILL START TO GET INTO IT, TOO.

HEAVY METAL HAS BEEN COOL FOR, LIKE, CENTURIES. BESIDES ALICE COOPER AND KISS, ROB HALFORD USED TO DRIVE A MOTORCYCLE ONSTAGE AND IRON MAIDEN HAD A DEAD DUDE NAMED EDDIE CHASING THEM AROUND. THESE DAYS, GWAR WEARS THESE HUGE COSTUMES AND GETS IN THESE BIG FIGHTS AND THERE'S BLOOD EVERYWHERE. IT'S LIKE, A MESSAGE OR SOME THING.

BUT ASSWIPES DON'T RESPECT HEAVY METAL AND IT PISSES COOL PEOPLE OFF. UNTIL SOMEBODY, LIKE, FINALLY GAVE METALLICA AN AWARD JUST SO THEY WOULDN'T GET THEIR ASS KICKED. NOW THE WHOLE WORLD REALIZES OR SOMETHING. . . HEAVY METAL RULES!!!

SOME RADIO DUDE SAID HEAVY METAL OWES A DEBT TO DUDES LIKE HENDRIX AND LED ZEPLIN. BEAVIS SAYS IT'S ONLY, LIKE, FIVE DOLLARS.

ALICE COOPER WAS THE FIRST DUDE TO DO COOL STUFF ONSTAGE. HE USED TO PLAY WITH SNAKES AND CUT OFF HIS HEAD. (GOOD THING HE DIDN'T PLAY WITH HIS HEAD AND CUT OFF HIS SNAKE. HUH, HUH!)

KISS WAS THE COOLEST, CAUSE NOBODY KNEW WHO THEY WERE, BUT, LIKE, EVERYBODY WANTED TO BE THEM. GENE SIMMONS EVEN SPIT BLOOD AND BREATHED, UH, STUFF. BEAVIS SPIT BLOOD AFTER I SMACKED HIM ONCE.

heavy metal

Ozzy bit the head off a bat just to show how cool he was. It worked. Beavis tried to do it but the bat bit him on the tongue and he got rabies again. What a dumbass!

AC/DC's singer sang "I'm on a Highway to Hell" and then he died. So he was, like, right. They got a new singer and I think he drives them around and stuff too.

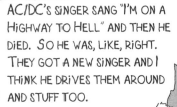

If Slash could see anything, he could look for a cool band to join.

If you're in Metallica, you're, like, not supposed to smile, cause they lost a Granny Award to Jethro Tull, and that really pissed them off. So they made an album that kicked even more ass and then they won. But they're still pissed.

Mm MEDICUL ADVISE

CONDISHUN	CURE
DINGLEBERRIES	TRY WIPING NEXT TIME
PATIENT IS PARALIZED	UNTIE STEWART
DIZZINESS, VOMITING	TURN OFF THE BON JOVI VIDEO
BLADDER PAIN	TAKE A WHIZ
HAIRY PALMS, LOSS OF EYESITE	GET RID OF YOUR MAGAZINE COLLECTION, BEAVIS
SCALY FLAKES OF DEAD SKIN FOUND ON SHOULDERS	QUIT SCRATCHING YOUR BUTT BEFORE YOUR PICK YOUR EARS
FREQUENT FARTING	GET THE HELL AWAY FROM ME
PENIS TOO SMALL	HUH HUH HUH HUH. YOU WUSS!

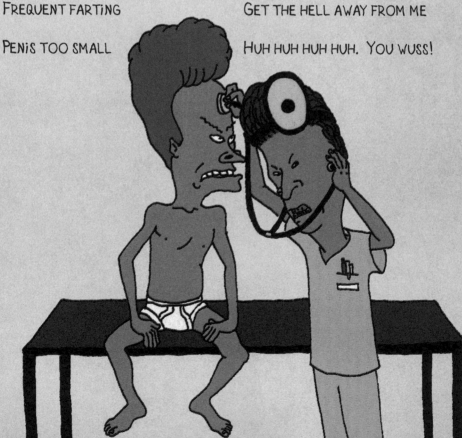

LLEWELYN, DOUG – THIS IS THAT DUDE FROM PEOPLE'S COURT WHO LIKE GIVES OUT THE PRIZES TO THE CONTESTANTS OR SOMETHING. AND, LIKE, WHAT THEY DON'T TELL YOU IS THAT IF YOU GO ON THE SHOW AND LOSE, WAPNER TELLS DOUG TO KICK YOUR ASS BEFORE HE SENDS YOU TO PRISON. JUSTICE IS COOL.

LOSERS – HEH HEH. THESE ARE DUDES WHO LIKE, THEY CAN'T GET CHICKS SO THEY GO HANG OUT IN FRONT OF THE MAXI-MART ON A FRIDAY NIGHT AND STUFF. UM, WE HANG OUT THERE TOO, BUT IT'S DIFFERENT CAUSE WE'RE ONLY THERE CAUSE THERE'S NOTHING GOOD ON TV ON FRIDAY NIGHTS.

LOVE – LOVE IS LIKE THIS CHEMICAL IN YOUR HEAD THAT MAKES YOU WANT TO HANG OUT WITH A CHICK EVEN IF, LIKE, YOU'RE NOT GONNA DO IT WITH HER SOON. THERE'S PROBLY PILLS AND STUFF THEY HAVE NOW THAT YOU CAN TAKE TO STOP THAT.

LOUD – LOUD IS LIKE THE PERFECT VOLUME FOR MUSIC. LIKE, IF YOU HAVE TO ASK, "IS THIS LOUD ENOUGH?" AND WE CAN LIKE HEAR YOU ASK IT, THEN YOU SHOULD TURN IT UP SOME MORE.

LUST – (SEE LOVE)

MAN-EATING – "MAN-EATING" IS LIKE THE BLACK BELT FOR ANIMALS. IT'S LIKE, ONLY ANIMALS LIKE A SHARK OR A VULTURE OR SOMETHING KICK ENOUGH ASS TO BE CALLED MAN-EATING. AND LIKE ANDERSON'S POODLE, WHO'S LIKE REAL OLD AND JUST LIKE LAYS AROUND A LOT, SHE'S MAYBE A YELLOW BELT ANIMAL. IF SHE'S LUCKY.

MARBLES – THESE ARE THESE THINGS YOU PUT IN YOUR NOSE WHEN YOU'RE A LITTLE KID AND THEN YOU GO TO THE HOSPITAL. THIS IS THEIR ONLY PURPOSE.

MEAT – HERE'S THE KIND OF MEAT WE CAN SHOW YOU. THE <u>ONLY</u> KIND, BEAVIS.

MICROWAVE – THIS IS A MACHINE THEY DEVELOPED DURING THE WAR TO LIKE FLY PLANES AND BLOW UP CITIES, AND NOW WE USE IT TO HEAT UP BURRITOS. SOMEBODY TOLD US THAT IF YOU STAND TOO CLOSE IT MAKES YOU SO YOU CAN'T HAVE BABIES, BUT THAT'S DUMB, CAUSE ONLY CHICKS HAVE BABIES.

MOMS – MOMS ARE COOL CAUSE THEY'RE ALWAYS LIKE GIVING YOU STUFF. FIRST, THEY GIVE YOU LIFE OR WHATEVER. THEN THEY GIVE YOU CLOTHES AND LIKE WALKING LESSONS OR SOMETHING. THEN, WHEN YOU'RE LIKE MATURE, THEY GIVE YOU TWENTY DOLLARS TO GET OUT OF THE HOUSE WHEN YOUR UNCLE COMES OVER. MOMS ARE COOL.

MONEY – IT USED TO BE THAT PEOPLE DIDN'T USE MONEY TO GET STUFF. LIKE, A GUY WHO WAS A NACHO FARMER, HE WOULDN'T SELL HIS NACHOS, HE'D JUST TRADE THEM FOR TVS OR SOMETHING. THEN, LIKE, HE'D TRADE A TV FOR CLOTHES. DUMBASS. BUT THEN PEOPLE GOT TIRED OF CARRYING TVS AROUND, SO THEY INVENTED MONEY, AND THE DUDES WHO INVENTED IT GOT TO HAVE THEIR PICTURES ON IT, WHICH WAS PRETTY COOL.

MUSTACHE – "MUSTACHE" IS LIKE FRENCH FOR "LIP BEARD." IT'S LIKE DIFFERENT FROM THE HAIR ON YOUR HEAD CAUSE YOU ONLY GET IT ONCE YOU GET YOUR TEST HORMONES. A LOT OF THE DUDES ON THAT COPS SHOW HAVE MUSTACHES. THEY MUST HAVE, LIKE, A LOT OF TEST HORMONES.

MUTANT – IF SOMETHING MESSES WITH A DUDE'S NATURAL STRUCTURE BEFORE HE'S BORN, HE BECOMES A MUTANT. THEN HE GOES FLYING AROUND KICKING ASS AND MEETING MUTANT CHICKS WHO WEAR COSTUMES THAT SHOW OFF THEIR THINGIES. ON THE OTHER HAND, IF A DUDE JUST GETS DROPPED ON HIS HEAD AS A BABY, HE BECOMES BEAVIS.

 **PETS**

PET	ADVANTAGES	DISADVANTAGES
DOG	* IF THERE'S ANOTHER DOG ON YOUR BLOCK, THEY'LL PROBABLY TRY AND DO IT, HUH HUH! * A DOG WILL SOMETIMES EAT ITS OWN VOMIT.	* WHEN IT WON'T EAT ITS OWN VOMIT, IT CAN BE REALLY HARD TO MAKE BEAVIS CLEAN UP THE COUCH.
CAT	* CAN BE TRAINED TO TAKE A DUMP IN A BOX. BEAVIS ENJOYED SHOWING THE STRAY CAT WE FOUND HOW TO DO IT.	* THE BOX GETS PRETTY GROSS AFTER A FEW WEEKS, UNLESS YOU ALSO HAVE ONE OF THOSE DUMBASS DOGS THAT LIKES TO SNACK OUT OF IT. UH, SHOULD THIS BE UNDER "DOG" OR SOMETHING? * NEUTERING A CAT CAN BE EXPENSIVE. AND YOU CAN ONLY HAVE IT DONE ONCE PER CAT.
GOLDFISH	* FLUSHABLE.	* IT TURNS OUT THEY DON'T REALLY HAVE ANY GOLD IN 'EM.
TURTLE	* THEY CAN'T GET AWAY SO EASY.	* WON'T EAT GOLDFISH.
BEAVIS	* YOU DON'T HAFTA PET HIM CAUSE, LIKE, HE PETS HIMSELF. HUH HUH. * IF YOU ALSO HAVE A DOG, YOU CAN FEED 'EM BOTH DOGFOOD.	* FLEAS. * MORE LIKELY TO FETCH A TURD THAN A STICK.
TAPEWORM	* YOU DON'T HAFTA BOTHER GOING ANYWHERE TO BUY IT OR FIND IT OR ANYTHING. A DOCTOR JUST ASKS FOR A TURD SAMPLE AND THEN TELLS YOU THAT YOU'VE GOT A PET TAPEWORM. * WHEN YOU HAVE ONE YOU CAN EAT A TON MORE NACHOS AND CANDY AND STUFF BEFORE YOU'RE FULL.	* THE DUMBASSES IN YOUR GYM CLASS WILL LAUGH AT YOU IF YOUR PET TAPE-WORM FALLS OUT WHEN YOU'RE DOING SQUAT THRUSTS. * ONCE IT FALLS OUT IT'S NOT COMING BACK. WITHOUT HELP, HUH HUH.
STEWART	* NONE. MAYBE PAY-PER-VIEW.	* WON'T RUN AWAY THE WAY SOME OTHER PETS DO.

Pp

THE PRESIDENTS OF THE U. S.

GEORGE DOLLAR	GEORGE ADAMS	GEORGE JEFFERSON
HE'S BALD. HUH HUH	SOME OTHER DUDE	STEVEN TYLER
CHRISTOPHER COLUMBUS	LINCOLN JEFFERSON	JFR
ELVIS, DUMBASS	MARTIN LUTHERING	THE OATMEAL GUY

THAT FELIX GUY

RINGO SOMETHING

GEORGE ADAMS
JEFFERSON

THE GUY FROM
THE 20

LIKE, A DOBERMAN
WOULDA BEEN GOOD

THAT FORIN DUDE

RONALD RAYMOND

DANIEL DAVE LEWIS

PRESIDENT SOMEBODY

UH, HE GOT BUSTED OR
SOMETHING

RONALD RAYMOND

MONT RUSHMORE

NORMAN STORM

RONALD RAYMOND

THE GUY WITH THE
COOL NAME

THE GUY FROM SCHOOL.
MCVICKER

Pp PAMPHLET WE GOT AT SCHOOL

P

Polite

H

Helpful

O

Opportunistic

N

Natural-sounding

E

Enterprisers

Opportunity Doesn't Knock —It Rings!!!

CAREER ROCK '94— IT'S FOR YOU!

Why are you here at Career Rock '94? Because your guidance counselors know you're ready for the fast track: the tough jobs in fields like food service, sanitation, and corrections. But why listen to their "authority-figure noise"…when you can start making the noise in a career with Jackpot Telemarketing, Inc.!

Before we get started, be warned. **If you hate making quick money while sitting in your favorite easy chair, STOP reading right now!** Try and earn your pay working in some dead-end job instead. (If you can!) Be careful, though—you might blow all of your hard-earned cash on some "get-rich-quick" scheme. Meanwhile, your friends who have a telemarketing career will be piling up the cash while *never* leaving their homes!

What's the difference? *Most get-rich-quick schemes* ***say*** *they're "sure things," but they really* ***aren't****. A telemarketing career* ***is.*** *Here's why:*

- **No risk.** Other salespeople have to buy shirts, ties, even hard shoes. You don't. You can be making money without even getting dressed!

At Jackpot Telemarketing, the only thing we want you to spend is time!

• **Big rewards.** We don't keep our employees tied down to a flat salary. They earn <u>unlimited</u> commissions! Just as long as you keep selling, you keep earning! Soon, you'll learn the money-making secret of the big corporations—volume. And you'll be putting it to work for you!

The phone is ringing—with opportunity. You can answer it, and say "Hello" to a fulfilling telemarketing career. Or you can hang up, and spend the rest of your life searching for fun and excitement. The phone is ringing—but it won't be ringing forever.

Beavis + Butt-head: Please implement soonest!

Burgut

Beavis, check it out he wrote "Plow"

PUT YOURSELF ON OUR PHONE!

We don't want you to leap into your exciting telemarketing career sight unseen. So here's a realistic sample of what to expect once you sign up with Jackpot Telemarketing:

Customer: Hello?
You: Hello, is [customer's name] at home?
Customer: Yes, this is [customer's name].
You: Hi, my name is [your name] from Jackpot Telemarketing. May I take some of your time to discuss an exciting financial opportunity?
Customer: Well, to be honest, I'm a little suspicious of telemarketers.
You: I understand. But when you hear about this exciting financial opportunity, you may feel quite differently.
Customer: Could you send something in the mail, please?
You: I could, [customer name], but by the time you received it, it would be too late to take advantage of this exciting financial opportunity.
Customer: You've convinced me. Tell me more.
[Later]
Customer: Thank you! Before, I didn't like telemarketing very much. But you've changed my mind. Please call me again if you have anything to offer.
You: I will. Thank you very much.

Note: Phrases such as "big money," "quick money," "easy money," and the like are not specific promises. Jackpot Telemarketing assumes no responsibility for telephone company charges you may incur. No representation is made by Jackpot Telemarketing concerning the efficacy or legality of products we may offer you to telemarket. Full liability, civil and otherwise, is assumed by the employee. Jackpot Telemarketing is no longer affiliated with Score Telemarketing, Pot O' Gold Telemarketing, Stretch Limo Telemarketing, or Lord's Way Cosmetics. As a matter of policy, Jackpot Telemarketing does not respond to customer or employee complaints.

Pp PUBLIC SERVANTS ANNOUNCEMENTS

LIKE, WHEN YOU'RE AS COOL AS WE ARE, PEOPLE WANT YOU TO MAKE THESE PUBLIC SERVANTS ANNOUNCEMENTS, SO LIKE LITTLE KIDS WON'T DO COOL STUFF OR SOMETHING. EXCEPT THEY HAVEN'T ASKED US YET, CAUSE THEY MUST BE SAVING US FOR SOMETHING IMPORTANT. SO, LIKE, JUST IN CASE, DO ALL THE STUFF WE SAY, AND LIKE DON'T DO ALL THE STUFF WE SAY DON'T. DO.

* LIKE, DO OTHERS THE WAY YOU WOULD WANT THEM TO DO YOU. HUH HUH HUH HUH.
* IF YOU'RE REALLY PISSED OFF AT SOMEBODY, COUNT TO TEN AFTER KICKING THEIR ASS.
* DON'T PET A STRANGE DOG UNLESS IT LOOKS LIKE IT MIGHT BITE YOU. THEN LIKE PET IT AND TRY TO MAKE FRIENDS WITH IT AND LIKE, GIVE IT A HUG.
* DON'T GET A FAKE ID. THEY NEVER WORK.
* IN CASE OF EMERGENCY, BREAK SOMETHING.
* ALWAYS KEEP A SPARE SET OF BATTERIES AROUND TO THROW AT BEAVIS.
* STAY IN SCHOOL, ESPECIALLY ON LIKE TACO DAY.
* DON'T LISTEN TO WINGER.
* MAKE SURE YOU PLAY YOUR STEREO LOUD TO DROWN OUT ANYONE WHO'S GONNA GIVE YOU CRAP ABOUT IT.

* IF YOU CAN'T SAY SOMETHING NICE ABOUT SOMEBODY, CALL THEM AN ASSWIPE.
* RESPECT YOURSELF.
* OH YEAH—MAKE SURE YOU WASH YOUR HANDS AFTER YOU RESPECT YOURSELF.
* UH, WHY DO YOU THINK THEY CALL BEAVIS DOPE, HUH HUH.
* SHUT UP, ASSWIPE. HEH HEH.
* DON'T EAT AT BURGER WORLD. WITH YOUR EYES OPEN, ANYWAY.
* DURING A TORNADO, DON'T GO ON THE ROOF WITHOUT A CAMERA.
* UH, HUH HUH HUH. DON'T DO IT WITH A CHICK UNLESS YOU'RE IN A CONDOMINIUM. HUH HUH HUH.
* UM, HEH HEH, DRIVE THROUGH, PLEASE.

Pp FUN WITH PLAYDOUGH

PLAYDOUGH IS COOL. YOU CAN PULL IT, AND POUND IT, AND ROLL IT BETWEEN YOUR HANDS. HUH HUH. SOMETIMES BEAVIS PLAYS POCKET PLAYDOUGH.

SHUT UP, BUTTMUNCH!

THE DIFFERENCE BETWEEN PLAYDOUGH AND, LIKE, YOUR MONKEY IS THAT WHEN YOU PLAY WITH IT IN CLASS, IT'S CALLED ART. HERE IS SOME OF MY AND BEAVIS'S BEST WORK WITH PLAYDOUGH. SOME OF IT WE EVEN GOT A GRADE ON.

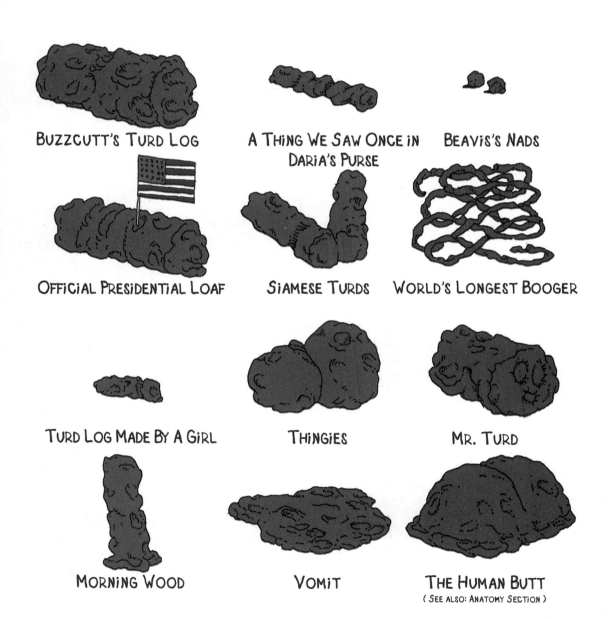

BUZZCUTT'S TURD LOG

A THING WE SAW ONCE IN DARIA'S PURSE

BEAVIS'S NADS

OFFICIAL PRESIDENTIAL LOAF

SIAMESE TURDS

WORLD'S LONGEST BOOGER

TURD LOG MADE BY A GIRL

THINGIES

MR. TURD

MORNING WOOD

VOMIT

THE HUMAN BUTT
(SEE ALSO: ANATOMY SECTION)

Rr APPLIANCE REPAIR

MOST PEOPLE DON'T KNOW HOW A TV WORKS. THAT'S WHY YOU GOTTA GO TO TECHKNOCKER COLLEGE. BUT EVEN THOUGH WE'RE NOT TECHKNOCKERS, WE'VE SEEN ENOUGH TV TO PRETTY MUCH KNOW HOW IT WORKS, AND WHAT YOU DO WHEN IT SCREWS UP.

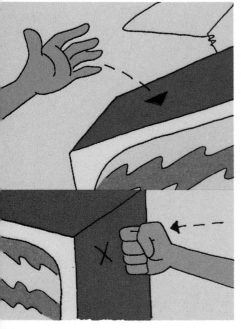

STEP 1 SMACKING AND POUNDING

TV PICTURES COME IN THROUGH THE WIRE AND HOOK UP WITH A LITTLE WIRE-SIZED TV INSIDE YOUR TV. THEN THE LITTLE PICTURE GETS BLOWN UP TO THE BIG PICTURE YOU SEE ON YOUR SCREEN. SO LIKE, A PICTURE OF AN EXPLOSION, IT GETS BLOWN UP TWICE, HUH HUH. THAT'S PRETTY COOL.

BUT ANYWAY, WHEN YOUR TV PICTURE IS MESSED UP, IT'S PROBLY BECAUSE ONE A THE KNOBS ON THE LITTLE TV IS MESSED UP. BUT DON'T OPEN THE TV TO TRY AND FIX IT CAUSE YOU'LL GET LECTRICUTED, AND THEN, EVEN AFTER THAT, IT'S TOO COMPLICATED. JUST SMACK IT. SMACK IT NOT SO HARD AT FIRST, THEN WORK YOUR WAY UP TO WHERE IT GETS FIXED.

YOU CAN WARM UP ON BEAVIS IF YOU WANT TO. HUH HUH HUH HUH.

AFTER A WHILE, IF YOU SMACKED IT RIGHT, AND YOUR TV'S NOT TOO MESSED UP, YOU'LL FIGURE OUT JUST WHERE IT'S GOTTA BE HIT TO FIX IT. IT'S LIKE ITS H-SPOT OR SOMETHING, HUH HUH. THAT'S WHEN YOU MOVE TO POUNDING IT WHEN IT'S BROKEN. MAKE A FIST, LIKE YOU'RE GONNA KICK SOMEONE'S ASS, BUT ONLY USE THE SIDE OF IT. IF LIKE YOU'VE BROKEN YOUR HAND TRYING TO FIX SOMETHING ELSE, USE A HAMMER.

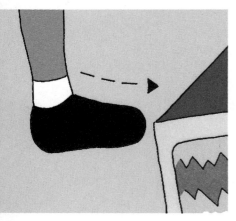

STEP 2 KICKING

SMACKING AND POUNDING IS UM THE METHOD RECOMMENDED BY DOCTORS OR WHATEVER, BUT SOMETIMES A TV WON'T LISTEN TO REASON, HEH HEH. THAT'S WHEN YOU GOTTA CALL IN THE BIG GUNS, EXCEPT THEY'RE FEET, NOT GUNS. KICK THE TV HARD, RIGHT IN THE NADS. AND, LIKE, IF YOUR TV DOESN'T HAVE NADS, THEN PRETEND IT DOES. KICK IT REALLY HARD. NO, HARDER THAN THAT, YOU WUSS. NAIL IT! NAIL IT! IF YOU'RE DOING IT RIGHT, THE TV SHOULD FALL OFF THE BOX OR WHATEVER YOU HAVE IT ON.

MOST OF THE TIME, KICKING DOESN'T WORK, BUT IT'S CAUSE NOTHING WOULDA FIXED THE TV ANYWAY, AND LIKE AT LEAST YOU TAUGHT IT A LESSON, HEH HEH.

OTHER APPLIANCES

MOST OTHER APPLIANCES, LIKE A REFRIGERATOR, OR, UH, A BOOK, AREN'T LIKE AS COMPLICATED AS TVS. SO THERE'S LIKE NO USE TRYING TO SMACK THEM, CAUSE IT WON'T HAVE ANY EFFECT. KICKING MIGHT WORK, IF YOU HAVE LIKE GOOD BOOTS, BUT OUR PROFESSIONAL ADVICE IS TO JUST THROW WHATEVER IT IS OUT AND GO BACK TO WATCHING TV.

Rr PERMANENT RECORD

UM, THIS WAS IN OUR PERMANENT RECORD, HEH HEH.
GUESS IT'S NOT REALLY PERMANENT.

LYNDON BAINES JOHNSON ELEMENTARY SCHOOL

To All Our New, Substitute, and Student Teachers:

I know there are a lot of questions you have about the procedures and customs here at L.B.J. Elementary. But I'm going to skip over all of those questions in the interest of going directly to your two biggest concerns.

Beavis and Butt-head are not to be trusted out of your sight. They are not to be trusted in your sight. You must never allow them to get behind you. Do not let them approach you at the same time. Do not "pull their fingers," even if Beavis cries. If they do come to your desk, together or separately, make them stay three to four feet away from it. If possible, stand up and keep your chair between you and them. At all times, be aware of the shortest exit path. Do not give them scissors. Do not give them rulers. They should not have glue, pens, erasers, paper or pencils. Ask them to remove their shoelaces when they enter your class. If possible, invite them to sleep through class. Avoid encouraging them to speak. Avoid speaking to them. If you must speak to them, do not be understanding, concerned, or "nice." Discourage others in your class from befriending or in any way helping them. Keep them apart from the others. If you can, put them in a box. Tell them it is a new learning tool from space. Keep the box sealed and instruct them not to laugh or speak as oxygen is limited. Tell the others it is really a box for very sick people and that they should not get close as they, too, may get sick. Pile several desks around the box. Leave the classroom with the others. Do not look back. Lead the others to the gym and hold class there. Barricade the doors.

Teaching is a rewarding, though demanding, profession. In the past few years, too many talented young teachers have decided that the demands outweigh the rewards. I hope, however, that by following these few simple guidelines, the trend can be reversed.

Sincerely,
Ms. Anne Camfey
Second Grade Teacher
L.B.J. Elementary School

RADIO

Free -Take One

KJWM (Highland's
Classic Hit Machine)
Program Guide

ON-AIR

Monday	Tuesday	Wednesday
6-10AM Ian and Larry in the Morning. I Hate Mondays. Larry crank calls the bosses of KJWM listeners. Plus a tape of Dan O'Keefe at his weekly alcoholics support group	6-10AM Ian and Larry in the Morning. I Hate Tuesdays. Larry crank calls the spouses and children of bosses of KJWM listeners	6-10AM Ian and Larry in the Morning. Hump Day! Ian and Larry crank call the clients and customers of the businesses KJWM listeners work for. Plus a tape of Dan O'Keefe soliciting a prostitute
10AM-2PM Bobby Cool. Lunchbreak: "Where are they now?" Today: Jimi Hendrix	10AM-2PM Bobby Cool. Lunchbreak: "KJWM RockVault" Today: Thirty minutes of "Freebird"	10AM-2PM Bobby Cool. Lunchbreak: "KJWM Komedy Klub" Today: Louie Anderson on being different
2-6PM Dan O'Keefe's Afternoon Soundoff. Live Call-In. Today: Is the media killing America?	2-6PM Dan O'Keefe's Afternoon Soundoff. Live Call-In. Today: Morning Radio—enemy of Democracy?	2-6PM Dan O'Keefe's Afternoon Soundoff. Live Call-In. Today: Is management ignoring the fact that people here want to ruin me?
6-10PM The Rock'n'Roll Whore! KJWM's Sheila Delmuzzo plays bands she knows "intimately." Tonight: Sam and Dave	6-10PM The Rock'n'Roll Whore! KJWM's Sheila Delmuzzo plays bands she knows "intimately." Tonight: Three Dog Night	6-10PM The Rock'n'Roll Whore! KJWM's Sheila Delmuzzo plays bands she knows "intimately." Tonight: The Dave Clark 5
10PM-12AM Sextalk with Dr. Joy. Being your own best friend. Concerns, questions, getting started	10PM-12AM Sextalk with Dr. Joy. How could it be wrong when it feels so right? Knowing where and when to be your own best friend	10PM-12AM Sextalk with Dr. Joy. Ten signs that say you need to give being your own best friend a break
12-6AM Bob Atherton's Nightowls. As an unpaid intern, Bob has been instructed not to speak on the air. Please report him if he fails to comply	12-6AM Bob Atherton's Nightowls. If you are unhappy with the selections Bob plays, report him immediately to Hit Machine management and he will be dealt with	12-6AM Bob Atherton's Nightowls. Bob thinks that because he is a radio major he knows more about radio than anybody here. But he doesn't. Report him

"Greetings, people of Highland. Don't forget to enter the Classic Hit Machine's Royal Pain in the Ass Contest. Just send your name, address and number on a postcard addressed to me, Rocko, the Classic Hit Machine Robot, and if you're entry is chosen, we'll broadcast Ian and Larry in the Morning from your home.

Thursday	Friday	Saturday	Sunday
6-10AM Ian and Larry in the Morning. Take this Job and Shove It. Ian crank calls the same bosses Larry crank called on Monday	**6-10AM** Ian and Larry in the Morning. T.G.I.F. Larry and Ian crank call the families, co-workers, bosses and clients of KJWM listeners. Plus a tape of Dan O'Keefe's humiliating testimony in divorce court	**6-10AM** Welcome to the Weekend. KJWM intern Bob Atherton with four hours of solid rock. You don't want to sleep through this! But don't beat yourself up if you do	**6-10AM** Rock, Roll, Redemption. Rev. Stiv Razor preaches a message of love through Christian rock
10AM-2PM Bobby Cool. Lunchbreak: "Request Line" Today: Anything by Emerson, Lake & Palmer	**10AM-2PM** Bobby Cool. Lunchbreak: "Block Party Friday" Today: Twelve in a row from Yes	**10AM-2PM** Revolution. Beatle-ographer Peter Delmarco. Today: "Norwegian Wood"—36 alternate takes	**10AM-2PM** Soaptown Bob Atherton spins the hits you love washing your car to! As an intern, Atherton is not allowed to speak on the air. Report him if he does
2-6PM Dan O'Keefe's Afternoon Soundoff. Live Call-In. Today: Ian and Larry—suspension or prison?	**2-6PM** Dan O'Keefe's Afternoon Soundoff. Live Call-In. Today: What to listen to when one KJWM dj is in prison and two others are dead	**2-6PM** KJWM Listener Poll's Top 3 Million Rock Songs Countdown. Today: numbers 2,345,695 through 2,345,634. Compiled by Bob Atherton	**2-6PM** Styx and Stones. A random selection of hits representing the spectrum of quality. Compiled by Bob Atherton
6-10PM The Rock'n'Roll Whore! KJWM's Sheila Delmuzzo plays bands she knows "intimately." Tonight: Take 6	**6-10PM** The Rock'n'Roll Whore! KJWM's Sheila Delmuzzo plays bands she knows "intimately." Tonight: The Moody Blues with the London Symphony Orchestra	**6-10PM** Listener Poll Top 3 Million Songs, continued. Songs 2,345,634 through 2,345,575	**6-10PM** Whatever! Grizzled Rock Veteran Vince Skulty plays obscure, unlistenable music, and rambles pointlessly for long intervals. Check it out!
10PM-12AM Sextalk with Dr. Joy. First aid for abrasions and blisters. Have I permanently ruined my best friend?	**10PM-12AM** Sextalk with Dr. Joy. What to do while your best friend is healing, a preview of tomorrow's KJWM Listener Poll Top 3 Million Rock Songs Countdown	**10PM-12AM** Listener Poll Top 3 Million Songs, continued. Songs 2,345,575 through 2,345,545	**10PM-12AM** Hello, Highland. Public forum hosted by Dr. Ron Quiring. Tonight: The General Trend Toward Rising Cancer Rates in the Tri-County Area and the implementation of the new Incinerator—Are They Related?
12-6AM Bob Atherton's Nightowls. Bob Atherton took out KJWM executive secretary Molly Carlson but he forgot his wallet and now he doesn't even say hi. He should be fired except he's just an intern	**12-6AM** Bob Atherton's Nightowls. And if Bob Atherton doesn't call me soon, he's gonna deal with my brothers, one of whom wrestled at 170 for Highland	**12-6AM** Bob Atherton's Nightowls. When a person gives herself up to you in a intimate way, and then you take 13 dollars for a cab out of her purse while she's still sleeping, you're not being respectful	**12-6AM** Bob Atherton's Nightowls. Do not have margueritas with Bob Atherton. His penis is bent and has a mole on it. Like a growth. Plus, it's very, very small. He is a dog

That's right, they'll come to your house, broadcast from your bedroom, and use your phone to crank call Buckingham Palace, home of the Queen of England! But hurry up and enter—this is our most exciting contest ever! Beep, spleep, biddy-biddy-bleep! This is Rocko, saying Rock On!"

QUIET – THE OPPOSITE OF "ROCK." I GUESS IT'S LATIN FOR "SUCK" OR SOMETHING. IT'S LIKE WHEN YOU'RE SPOSED TO SHUT UP AND LET OTHER PEOPLE LIVE IN PEACE, OR WHATEVER, EVEN IF THE OTHER PEOPLE'S QUIET IS AS LOUD TO YOU AS YOUR NOISE WOULD BE TO THEM, OR VICE VERSA. EITHER WAY, IT SUCKS.

QUICK – (SEE KWIK)

QUIZ – THIS IS A THING THEY DO AT SCHOOL THAT SUCKS MORE THAN HOMEWORK, BUT DOESN'T SUCK AS MUCH AS A TEST. VAN DRIESSEN SAYS IT'S JUST SOMETHING TO MAKE SURE WE'RE LISTENING IN CLASS. BUT IT'S LIKE, IF THAT'S ALL YOU NEED TO KNOW, WHY DON'T YOU JUST ASK US IF WE'RE LISTENING. LIKE, IT TAKES US A LOT LESS TIME TO SAY NO THAN TO FAIL A STUPID QUIZ.

QUALITY – THEY PUT THIS BIG "THINK QUALITY!" SIGN UP AT BURGER WORLD ONE TIME. BUT WE DIDN'T PAY TOO MUCH ATTENTION TO IT CAUSE IT SAID "THINK" AND STUFF, AND THEN THEY TOOK IT DOWN AFTER ALL THE NEWSPAPER ARTICLES. MAYBE IT WAS SOME KIND OF NEW BURGER THEY WERE PLANNING, BUT THEY NEVER EXPLAINED TO US WHAT IT MEANT, SO IT MUST HAVE TASTED BAD OR SOMETHING.

RABIES – YOU CAN GET RABIES FROM A DOG BITE. BUT NOT EVERY DOG BITE, CAUSE I LIKE EXPEARMINTED ON BEAVIS, AND MOST OF THE TIME, WHEN YOU'RE SPOSED TO LIE DOWN AND LIKE FOAM AT THE MOUTH, HE JUST RAN AROUND SCREAMING. THEN ONE TIME HE THOUGHT HE HAD IT AND HE BIT ME. THAT'S WHEN I HAD TO GIVE HIM SOME SHOTS FROM DR. KNUCKLE SANDWICH.

RATS – RATS ARE LIKE THE SHARKS OF THE ANIMAL KINGDOM. THEY JUST TAKE WHAT THEY WANT, AND NOBODY GETS IN THEIR WAY, SPECIALLY CAUSE WHAT THEY WANT IS GARBAGE. IT WOULD BE COOL TO HAVE A RAT AS A DOG, CAUSE THEN YOU WOULDN'T HAVE TO BUY IT RAT CHOW OR WHATEVER AND PLUS THE ANIMAL PEOPLE WOULDN'T CARE IF YOU LIKE DID SCIENCE ON IT, HEH HEH HEH.

REMOTE – SOMETIMES YOU SEE OLD TVs AT LIKE A YARD SALE WITH THESE KNOBS ON THEM AND YOU'RE LIKE, "WHOA, NO REMOTE, WHAT'S THE DEAL?" BACK IN THOSE DAYS, THEY SAY, YOU HAD TO LIKE GET UP AND GO OVER TO THE TV TO CHANGE IT. LIKE, IT WAS ALMOST LESS WORK TO STUDY THAN TO WATCH TV. SO THE REMOTE IS LIKE A GREAT INVENTION, SINCE NOW YOU CAN CHANGE IT FROM A SHOW THAT SUCKS INTO ONE THAT ALSO SUCKS, ONLY NOT AS MUCH.

ROACH MOTEL – THIS ONE SHOULD BE SIMPLE. IT'S JUST LIKE A ROACH TRAP, RIGHT? IT'S LIKE THE PRISON FOR THE BUGS WHO DON'T GET SENTENCED TO DEATH. BUT PEOPLE GET CONFUSED. LIKE ONE TIME DARIA CALLED OUR COUCH A BIG ROACH MOTEL, EVEN THOUGH THERE WAS A WHOLE BOX OF 'EM THE SOCIAL WORKER HAD GIVEN US RIGHT WHERE SHE COULD SEE IT. AND THEY WEREN'T EVEN UNWRAPPED. DARIA'S NOT AS SMART AS PEOPLE THINK SOMETIMES.

ROCK – MUSIC ROCKS IF IT'S COOL AND IF, LIKE, THE LOUDER YOU PLAY IT, THE COOLER IT GETS. IF YOU THOUGHT IT WAS COOL AND THEN YOU PLAY IT LOUD AND IT SUCKS, THEN IT WAS PROBABLY COLLEGE MUSIC OR SOMETHING. OR, IF YOU THINK IT'S COOL, AND THEN YOU PLAY IT LOUD, AND YOU THINK IT SUCKS, AND THEN YOU PLAY IT LOUDER, AND IT SOUNDS COOL AGAIN, THEN SOMETHING'S WRONG WITH YOUR STEREO OR MAYBE THE SONG JUST HAS A SUCKY PART, LIKE A LOT OF THEM DO.

Ss SPORTS

SPORTS ARE STUPID, CAUSE THEY MAKE YOU EXERCISE, AND YOU CAN'T DO 'EM UNLESS YOU'VE GOT LIKE TEN OTHER GUYS AND A FOOTBALL STADIUM OR SOMETHING.

ME AND BEAVIS FIGURED OUT THAT THE MOST IMPORTANT THING IN SPORTS IS THAT YOU SCORE, HUH HUH. SO WE STARTED MAKING UP SPORTS THAT WERE COOLER AND FUNNER.

BREAKING STUFF -
YOU JUST TAKE STUFF AND YOU BREAK IT. AND YOU GET POINTS FOR EACH PIECE. LIKE IF IT BREAKS INTO FIVE PIECES, YOU GET, LIKE, I GUESS IT WOULD BE FIVE POINTS.

THROWING OUT THE GARBAGE -
YOU GET LIKE A LOT OF GARBAGE, AND YOU STAND ABOUT TWENTY FEET FROM THE TRASH CAN, AND YOU THROW GARBAGE AT IT. IF YOU GET IT IN, YOU GET TWO POINTS. IF YOU MISS, YOU GO WATCH TV.

FLY TENNIS -
OPEN ALL YOUR DOORS AND WINDOWS SO FLIES CAN GET IN THE HOUSE. THEN KILL THEM WITH A TENNIS RACKET. EACH FLY IS WORTH 15 POINTS.

WHO CAN STAY AWAKE THE LONGEST-
TRY TO STAY AWAKE AS LONG AS YOU CAN. YOU GET A POINT FOR

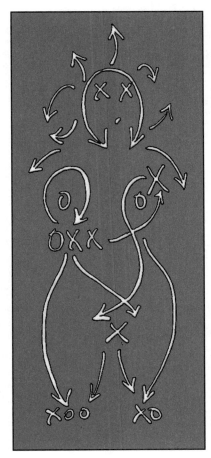

EVERY HOUR YOU STAY AWAKE. THE FIRST ONE TO FALL ASLEEP IS A WUSS.
(SEE ALSO: SLEEP DEPRIVASHUN)

SPITTING FOOD -
JUST LIKE PUT SOME FOOD IN YOUR MOUTH AND SPIT IT AT STUFF. IF YOU HIT IT, YOU GET A POINT.

LONG DISTANCE PEEING -
SEE HOW FAR YOU CAN STAND FROM THE TOILET AND STILL GET MOST OF YOUR PEE IN IT. OR AT LEAST SOME. PEE. AFTER YOU GET REALLY GOOD, TRY TAKING A LONG DISTANCE DUMP. ONE POINT FOR NUMBER ONE, TWO POINTS FOR NUMBER TWO.

THROWING STUFF -
YOU JUST PICK UP STUFF AND THROW IT AS HARD AS YOU CAN. WE HAVEN'T FIGURED OUT HOW YOU SCORE POINTS, BUT IT'S STILL PRETTY COOL.

SLAMMING THE DOOR -
I TAKE ONE DOOR AND BEAVIS TAKES ANOTHER DOOR. WE TAKE TURNS SLAMMING IT AS HARD AS WE CAN. WHOEVER SLAMS IT THE LOUDEST GETS A POINT. THE FIRST ONE TO A THOUSAND POINTS WINS.

FIGHTING -
LIKE, WHENEVER I GET BORED, I JUST SMACK BEAVIS IN THE FACE. AND I KEEP HITTING HIM UNTIL HE HITS ME BACK. THEN, WE'RE LIKE, IN A FIGHT. EVERY TIME I PUNCH BEAVIS, IT'S WORTH A POINT. EVERY TIME I KICK HIM IN THE NADS, IT'S WORTH TWO POINTS. THE ONLY PROBLEM IS THAT I ALWAYS KICK BEAVIS'S ASS, AND THEN HE DOESN'T WANT TO PLAY ANY MORE SPORTS. SO YOU SHOULD SAVE THIS FOR LIKE YOUR FINAL EVENT OR SOMETHING.

This sewer pipe is cool. But it would be cooler if it was real small, so the stuff can shoot out really fast. Government is stupid.

Ss SEWERS

SEWERS ARE COOL CAUSE THEY'RE A HIGHWAY FOR TURDS, HEH HEH. IT'S LIKE, WHEN YOU FLUSH, YOU'RE SAYING, BYE, LITTLE FELLA, HAVE A NICE TRIP, SO LONG. MOST PEOPLE, AFTER THEY SAY BYE OR WHATEVER, THEY DON'T EVEN THINK LIKE WHERE THE TURD'S GOING. NOT US. LIKE, WE'RE ALWAYS THINKING ABOUT THAT KIND OF STUFF, HEH HEH. WE'RE NATURALLY INQUISITOR.

* BEFORE SEWERS PEOPLE JUST PINCHED LOAFS IN THE WOODS OR SOMETHING, HEH HEH. (SEE ALSO: TOILET, ILLUSTRATED) AND THEN THEY SAID, IT'S TOO FAR TO WALK, I'LL JUST GO IN THE PIPE. AND THEN IN A LITTLE WHILE, SOMEBODY POURED WATER IN THE PIPE, PROBLY BY ACCIDENT, AND LIKE, PRIESTO, SEWER. A LOT OF INVENTIONS AND STUFF GET INVENTED BY ACCIDENT. LIKE THE LECTRIC GUITAR, THE FIRST GUY JUST FOLLOWED THE CORD FROM THE OUTLET, AND HE WAS LIKE, HM, I'LL BE DAMNED, IT'S A GUITAR.

* IT'S COOL TO MAKE VIDEOS IN SEWERS CAUSE THEY DRIP WATER, WHICH IS LIKE COOL IN A VIDEO. NO ONE KNOWS WHY IT'S COOL, OR WHO DECIDED IT, BUT IT IS. AND PLUS LIKE PEOPLE THINK SEWERS SUCK, WHICH IS COOL FOR BANDS THAT THINK LIFE SUCKS, BUT THEY LOOK COOL, SEWERS I MEAN, AND ALL BANDS TRY TO LOOK COOL, EVEN LIKE THE ONES THAT THINK LOOKING COOL SUCKS.

* A LONG TIME AGO, THIS LITTLE KID FLUSHED THIS FAMILY OF SEA MONKEYS DOWN THE TOILET. AND NOW THEY LIVE THERE AND LIKE EAT HUBCAPS AND STRAY DOGS AND STUFF, THOUGH MOST OF THE TIME THEY PROBLY LIVE OFF TURDS TOO, I GUESS.

* SEWERS USUALLY END IN A RIVER OR A LAKE OR A TREATMENT PLANT OR SOME OTHER PLACE. A TREATMENT PLANT IS THIS PLACE WHERE THEY LIKE TREATMENT THE TURDS SO THEY DON'T GROSS PEOPLE OUT. LIKE, IN OUR TOWN, THEY ADD THIS OILY STUFF THAT GIVES THE WATER THIS BURNED SMELL. IT'S COOL, AND YOU CAN GET OUT OF SCHOOL IF YOU TELL VAN DRIESSEN YOU DRANK SOME.

* THIS ONE TIME A RAT CRAWLED OUT OF A SEWER AND DIED RIGHT IN FRONT OF US. IT WAS COOL.

* ANOTHER TIME THE SEWER DUDES LEFT THEIR MANHOLE COVER OPEN SO WE CHECKED IT OUT. IT KICKED ASS. WE WERE GONNA CLIMB ALL THROUGH THE SEWER SYSTEM AND CHECK OUT EVERYBODY'S TOILET, BUT BUTT-HEAD FELL IN SOME CRAP AND HE SAID WE HAD TO GET OUT BEFORE WE SET OFF THE WARNING SYSTEM OR WHATEVER. SO WE DEFINITELY KNOW THAT LIKE SEWERS HAVE GOOD SECURITY.

Ss SLEEP DEPRIVASHUN EXPEARMINT

22 May

10:00 P.M. Me and Beavis decide to try staying up all night. It's, like, a good skill to have, cause night is when most chicks do it. If you're gonna score you gotta know how to stay up late. And how to "stay up" late. Huh huh huh huh.

10:29 P.M. We each drank twelve sodas to be sure and stay awake all night. We figure it'll be hard to fall asleep if we hafta keep getting up to take a whiz.

10:47 P.M. M HEH HEH HEH HEH. THAT LINE ABOUT "STAY UP" LATE WAS PRETTY FUNNY. BUTT-HEAD JUST EXPLAINED IT TO ME.

11:04 P.M. Nighttime T.V. sucks. There's nothing on but a bunch of fartknocking shows about the news, or something.

11:38 B.M.

Huh huh, that's "p.m.", dumbass!

NO WAY, BUTT-HEAD, IT'S B.M.! M HEH HEH, I TOOK A DUMP AT 11:38. OH YEAH, I ALMOST FORGOT THE OTHER THING I DID...

11:39 P. HEH HEH HEH HEH.

12:00 A.M. THE STROKE OF MIDNIGHT.

12:23 A.M. THE STROKE OF 12:23.

12:47 A.M. THE STROKE OF ——————

Dammit Beavis, no-one wants to read about that!

OH YEAH. HEH HEH. SORRY ABOUT THAT. I GOT THIS DIARY CONFUSED WITH MY MONKEY-SPANKING DIARY.

2:30 A.M. Late night television sucks! Most stashuns have a sucky band playing the National Anthem, and now they're showing nothing but a bunch of static.

3:31 A.M. Watching the static on T.V. gets kind a boring after awhile.

3:39 A.M. WHOA! Heh Heh Heh, if you STAIR AT THE STATIC ON TV LONG ENOUGH, you START HALLOOCINATING, AND THEN YOU CAN SEE A NAKED CHICK FLOATING THERE. NAKED CHICKS RULE!

3:48 a.m. I've been trying to halloocinate from looking at the T.V. but I can't even get like dizzy. When Beavis thought he was halloocinating from watching the static, he musta been, like really halloocinating, or something.

3:53 a.m. I just remembered that Stewart said we could go over anytime and play with his new video game.

4:29 a.m. Stewart lied to us. We'll hafta kick his butt tomorrow. Or cane him. Huh huh huh huh. That would be cool.

4:45 A.M. EH HEH HEH. First offisttul SIGN of MORNING. I HAVE MORNING WOOD! HEH HEH M HEH.

5:18 a.m. Beavis ackshully got a smart idea. We could call up one of those 24-hour phone sex chicks now, when she'll probably be in bed and extra horny.

5:35 a.m. All she wanted to talk about was, like, "Do you have a credit card and what's the number on it?" We couldn't remember what we did with Anderson's credit card, so I hanged up. But then Beavis was really pissed off. Huh huh huh! He was getting a woodrow just talking about credit cards with the chick. Fartknocker!

5:36 A.M. DUMBASS!

5:37 a.m. Shut up Beavis, you turdwipe!

5:38 A.M. EH HEH H He HIM, DILLHOLE!

5:39 a.m. Don't make me kick your ass. Beavis.

5:40 A.M. BUTT-HOLE!

5:41 a.m. I kicked Beavis's ass, huh huh huh. I punched him so hard he fell asleep.

5:42 a.m. Early morning T.V. sucks.

(SOMETHING IN) MY PANTS

THERE'S SOMETHING IN MY PANTS
THERE'S SOMETHING IN MY PANTS
THERE'S SOMETHING IN MY PANTS
AND I THINK IT'S GROWING.

I DON'T KNOW WHAT MAKES IT GROW
THE WAY YOU LOOK, THE CLOTHES
  YOU WEAR
MY HAND IN MY POCKET, YOUR SMELL
  IN THE AIR
ALL I KNOW IS IT'S GOT TO BE FREE
GOTTA GET SOMETHING STRAIGHT
  BETWEEN YOU AND ME

CHORUS
THERE'S SOMETHING IN MY PANTS
THERE'S SOMETHING IN MY PANTS
THERE'S SOMETHING IN MY PANTS
AND I THINK IT'S GROWING.

(REPEAT CHORUS. REPEAT AGAIN.)
YEAH. IT IS.

IF I SAID I LOVE YOU

WOULD YOU TAKE OFF YOUR SHIRT IF
  I SAID THE WORDS?
WOULD YOU?
IF I SAID I LOVE YOU, WOULD YOU, LIKE,
  JUST TAKE OFF THE SHIRT?
WOULD YOU?

BECAUSE, BABY, IF THAT'S WHAT IT
  TAKES TO PROVE I WANT TO SEE YOU
  WITHOUT A SHIRT,
I'LL SAY IT.
I MEAN, IF LIKE, THE ONLY WAY I'LL SEE YOU
  WITHOUT YOUR SHIRT IS TO SAY
  I LOVE YOU,
I'LL SAY IT.

IF YOU TOOK OFF YOUR SHIRT BEFORE
  I EVEN SAID IT, THOUGH,
THAT WOULD BE COOL. SAVE ME
  SOME TROUBLE OR SOMETHING.
BUT REALLY, LIKE, IF THE ONLY WAY TO
  GET YOU OUT OF THE SHIRT IS TO SAY IT,
THAT'S COOL, TOO.

BECAUSE, BABY, THE IMPORTANT THING IS TO
  GET YOUR SHIRT OFF.
GET YOUR SHIRT OFF.
LIKE, THE IMPORTANT THING IS TO GET THAT
  DAMN THING OFF.
YEAH, GET IT OFF.

HAPPY TUNE

HUH HUH HUH
HUH HUH.

UH HUH HUH HUH.
HUH HUH HUH.

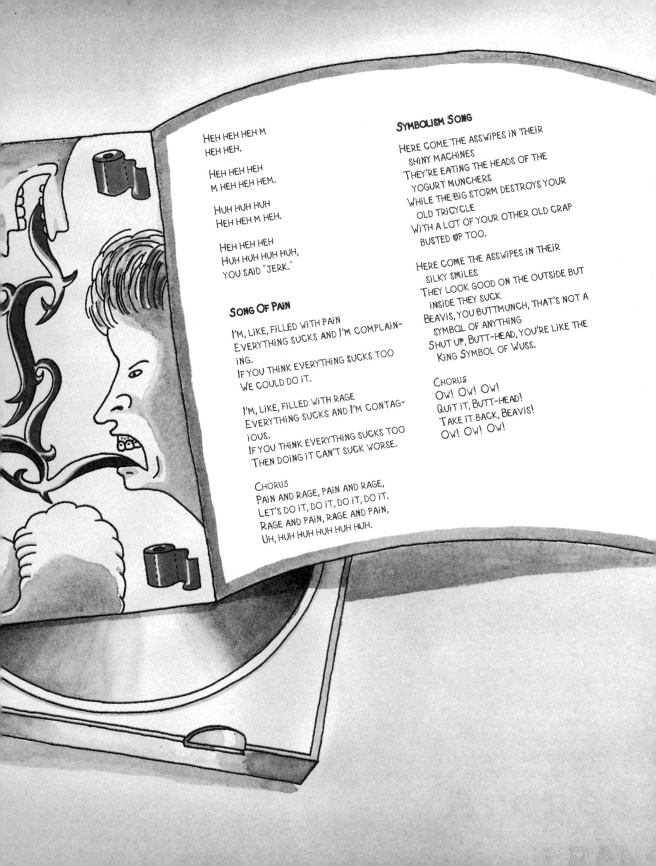

HORSES CAN TAKE A DUMP WHILE THEY'RE WALKING, BUT THEY HAFTA STAND IN ONE PLACE TO PEE.

IT'S FIZZICALLY IMPOSSIBLE TO CHOKE YOUR CHICKEN MORE TIMES IN ONE DAY THAN THE NUMBER OF YEARS OLD YOU ARE. BEAVIS CAN'T WAIT UNTIL HIS FIFTEENTH BIRTHDAY.

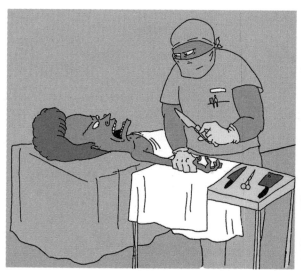

IF YOU AMPUTATE AN INSECT'S LEG, IT'LL KEEP MOVING, EVEN THOUGH IT'S NOT ATTACHED TO THE INSECT ANYMORE. HUH HUH HUH! AND IF YOU, LIKE, AMPUTATE BEAVIS'S HAND? IT'LL PROBABLY KEEP SPANKING HIS MONKEY.

BEAVIS SAYS HE KICKED MY ASS ONCE. IT MUSTA BEEN WHILE I WAS ASLEEP, OR I WOULDA KICKED HIS ASS INSTEAD.

BUTT TRUE

Some dudes ackshully freeze their sperm. Beavis prefers to make his fresh daily.

There's, like, these chicks that'll do it with you if you pay them enough money. Even Beavis.

A hundred years ago, in, like, the Dark Ages, people's bathing suits covered practically their whole bodies. Even chicks' bathing suits. The Dark Ages sucked!

One day Beavis is gonna grow up to be a man. Believe it or not, he might even score then. Uh, see above.

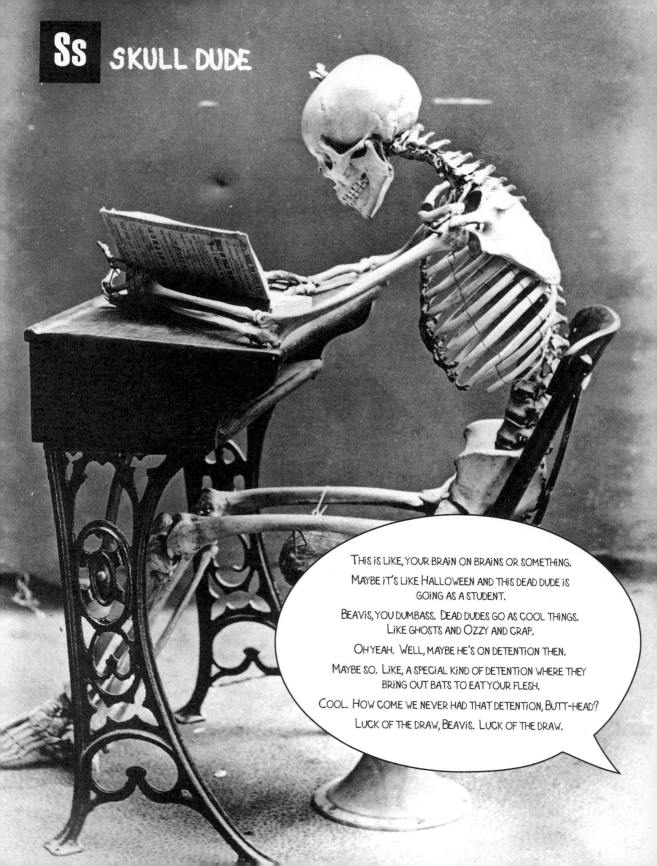

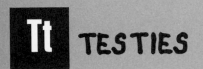

TESTIES

THE TRICK TO TAKING A TEST IS TO ANSWER EVERY QUESTION, EVEN IF THE QUESTION SUCKS. BEAVIS
ACKSHULLY GOT A C- ONE TIME ON ONE OF VAN DRIESSEN'S TESTS THIS WAY.

TEST SHEET
Mr. Van Driessen's Class
Week Seven Test
Subject: The U.S. and Central America.

C-

Good Work, Beavis I sense that you're really making some progress

List the states of Central America.

Mississississippi, Houston, England and Nicaragua. Nicaragua! Aqua!

Which overly aggressive American leader summed up his belligerent policy
towards Central America with the phrase, "Speak softly and carry a big stick"?

THAT WAS PROBLY ME OR SOMETHING ESPESHULLY THE PART ABOUT THE BIG STICK.

What were President Kennedy's interventionist goals in going forward with
the disastrous "Bay of Pigs" invasion in 1961?

UH, ME AND BUTT-HEAD FOUND A PIG ONCE ON SOME OLD DUDES FARM. IT WAS EATING
A BUNCH OF GARBAGE. WE WERE, UH, WORRIED ABOUT THE PIG, HAVING ALL THAT BAD FOOD IN IT, AND STUFF?
SO WE FED IT SOME LEFTOVER CHOCLAT LACKSATIVES FOR, LIKE SIENCE.

What was the outcome?

A BIG TURD. ITS OUTCOME WAS SO FAST I GOT SPLATTERED. THAT SUCKED!

Compare and contrast the soaring rhetoric of America's "Good Neighbor"
policy towards Central America with the grim reality of "Dollar Diplomacy."

UH, COULD YOU REPEAT THE QUESTION?

List a few ways in which the United States could truly be a "Good Neighbor"
to other countries in this hemisphere.

WE COULD SET OUR TAZERS ON STUN, UNLESS WE WERE, LIKE, REALLY ANGRY. WE COULD SEND THEM MORE
AMERICUNS, TO HELP THEM OUT SO THEY WOULDN'T BE SO FULL OF FOREINURZ. AND WE COULD DO IT WITH THEIR
CHICKS. THAT'D BE COOL!

CLARK COBB'S TOOL CHEST

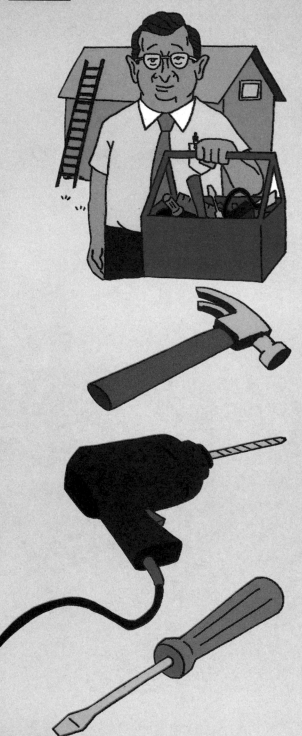

Hello, young students. I'm Clark Cobb of Cobb Family Hardware. Did you know Christ was a carpenter? That's right. And you better believe He took good care of his tools. At Cobb Family Hardware, we believe that a man who's got his toolbox in order is a man who's got his soul in order—just so long as he keeps in mind the words of Psalm 127: "Unless the Lord builds the house, those who build it labor in vain" (Verse 1). But you should also keep in mind the tenth Psalm, "Break thou the arm of the wicked and evil-doer." (Verse 15). Which is why in my book, like the Good Book, if a fella gets into your tools, you got the God-given right to break some arms.

Hammer Just as the Lord may use a tractor-trailer brake failure to pound a little faith into a car full of joyriding young people, so I use my hammer to pound nails into boards of wood. And like nails, faith holds this House of Man together. I call my hammer Big Rig.

Drill Folks, don't go to a job without the right tools. Sometimes, hammer and nails aren't enough. Many times I have gathered with my brethren CBs to assemble a large scaffold or stage from which to celebrate the occasion of a recently paroled minister or Businessman only to find that there are still those who have not heard the good news about drills, bolts and nuts. Listen up folks: get a drill.

Screwdriver Jesus once said to the Pharisees, "He who does not enter the sheepfold by the door but climbs in by another way, that man is a thief and a robber" (John 10:1). But you know what? Sometimes the door is broke! But with your screwdriver, you can take off the hinges, move the door, and go right in. Incidentally, I'm sure you'll all agree that in the above statement the Lord makes pretty damn clear his opinion of your so-called alternative lifestyles.

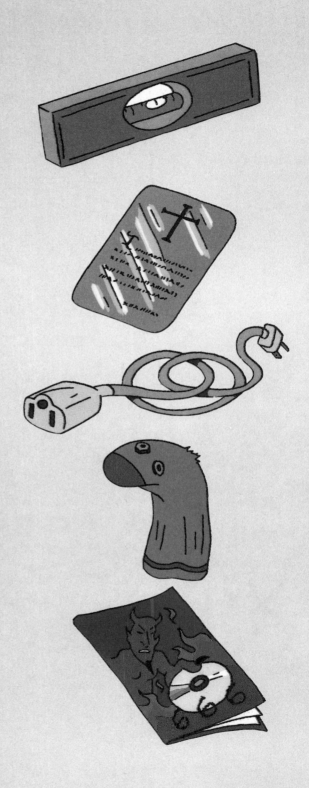

Level Sometimes in life, you need to step back and ask, "Am I on the level? Is my life straight and true?" As a guide, we may turn to our pastor, or to a fellow Christian Businessman. And that Christian Businessman may say, "Clark, you're sagging—let's get on our knees and get you straightened out." Well, think of a level as a Christian Businessman who's got a little bubble instead of a mouth.

Laminated Copy of the Christian Businessmen's Association Oath "I swear to do my best to spread the God's Report® while building business opportunities in the community. For as faith nourishes the soul, so good business nourishes the community in which the soul and its body live. I will not be unfair in my business, and I will profitshare with the Lord."

®God's Report is a registered trademark of the Christian Businessmen's Association. The Christian Businessmen's Association is a chartered member of Christworks, Inc., a division of the Wormwood Industries Group.

Extension Cord When I see a church steeple, I think of it as an extension cord to heaven, bringing the "juice" of the Lord right down into the little people like me. In a way, I think of myself as a little tiny robot man who gets his battery charged every Sunday down at First Highland Methodist. Then I run around all week like a robot until I start to wind down on Saturday. Sunday, I'm good as new.

Socko II Meet my friend, Socko II. He lives in my toolbox. It's good having a friend with you when you do your work. Because even though the Lord is always with you, sometimes, as in the book of Revelations, "there was silence in heaven" (Chapter 8, Verse 1). But if you put a friend in your toolbox, you can strike up a conversation any time you want. Socko II's brother, Socko, lives in the glove compartment of my vehicle. I take him out to talk to young students like you. And, sometimes, to me when I drive.

Pamphlets Often when I'm working with my tools, young people gather round to watch. That's why I keep these important youth-orientated pamphlets: "Help Me, Lord, My Body Is Changing"; "666 is Satan in Digital—CD's Every Youngster Should Avoid"; "God's Expectations For Dating"; "The Seven Warning Signals of Hell"; "Onan, Girls, and God—Where Do I Fit In?"; "Dear Jesus, Why Did Daddy Leave?—Children's Letters to Christ."

THE ILLUSTRATED TOILET

BEFORE THE TOILET WAS INVENTED, PEOPLE HAD NO PLACE TO GO TO THE TOILET.

THAT'S NOT TRUE, BUTT-HEAD. SOMETIMES THEY WENT OUTSIDE. WHEN PEOPLE ASKED THEM WHERE THEY WERE GOING, THEY SAID, LIKE, "I HAVE TO GO TO THE FOREST," OR, "I HAVE TO GO TO THE SIDEWALK."

OR IF THEY WERE LIKE YOU, BEAVIS, THEY SAID, "I HAVE TO GO TO MY PANTS." HUH HUH.

SHUT UP, BUTT-HEAD!

TODAY EVERYONE USES THE TOILET BUT NO ONE KNOWS HOW THEY WORK. EXCEPT ME AND BEAVIS. WE DID LIKE RESEARCH IN THE LIBRARY. IN THE TOILET SECTION. THE FIRST THING WE LEARNED WAS, WHEN YOU FLUSH A TOILET, IT MAKES THE TURD DISAPPEAR. HUH HUH. THAT WAS COOL! WE'RE GONNA START DOING THAT.

NOT ME.

BUT WE LEARNED MORE. WE WROTE IT ALL DOWN ON A DIAFRAM OF A TOILET SO YOU CAN LEARN IT TOO. ALL THIS STUFF IS TRUE. IF YOU DON'T BELIEVE IT, TRY FLUSHING A TOILET SOMETIME. THEN LIFT UP THE SEAT. LIKE, PRIESTO OR SOMETHING!

TOILET SEAT: PLACE YOUR BIG BUTT HERE.

TOILET BOWL: WHERE THE CRAP AND VOMIT GO. OH YEAH, AND WEE-WEE.

FLUSHER THINGIE: TURN THIS AND IT MAKES THE TURD GO AWAY. IF YOU KNOW ONLY ONE THING ABOUT A TOILET, THIS SHOULD BE IT. OR TO LIFT THE SEAT COVER.

REFRIGERATOR SECTION: THIS IS WHERE BEAVIS'S MOM KEEPS HER MEDICINE COLD.

BIG COPPER BALL: THIS IS LIKE KEY TO THE WHOLE OPERATION. AS THE WATER RUSHES IN, SCIENTIFIC STUFF MAKES THIS BALL RISE TO THE TOP. IT'S LIKE WHEN BEAVIS WETS THE BED, SOMETIMES HE ALSO GETS A WOODROW.

PIPES AND STUFF: WE'RE NOT SURE WHAT THIS STUFF DOES CAUSE IT'S SO DARK IN THERE. THEY SHOULD PUT A LIGHT IN THE TOILET SO YOU CAN SEE WHERE THE CRAP GOES.

FART RECYCLER (OPTIONAL): THIS DEVICE IS FOUND SOMETIMES IN YOUR FINER TOILETS. IT LIKE COLLECTS FART GAS AND CONVERTS IT TO CHEAP FUEL THAT THEY CAN SELL TO POOR COUNTRIES. YEAH, HEH HEH. THE TURD WORLD.

READING MATERIAL: IT'S GOOD TO HAVE LOTS OF MAGAZINES WITH CLEAR PICTURES OF INTERESTING PEOPLE WHO LIKE TO, YOU KNOW, DO IT. MAKE SURE THEY'RE THE KIND YOU CAN READ WITH ONE HAND, IN CASE YOU NEED YOUR OTHER HAND TO LIKE UH...HUH HUH...PULL YOUR FLUSHER.

Uu URANUS

URANUS IS LIKE THE FUNNIEST OF ALL THE PLANETS. LIKE, JUST SAYING THE NAME URANUS WITHOUT LAUGHING IS PROBLY THE HARDEST PART ABOUT BEING ONE A THOSE ASSNAUTS. HUH HUH, URANUS. HEH HEH HEH. BUT IT'S ALSO DANGEROUS, CAUSE ONE TIME WE WERE LAUGHING AT IT AND BUZZCUT MADE US LIKE, GIVE A REPORT ABOUT IT. HE SAID HE WISHED HE COULD GIVE US CORPORAL PUNISHMENT, BUT LIKE, I DON'T THINK HE'S ALLOWED TO CAUSE HE NEVER GOT THAT FAR IN THE MARINES.

FACTS ABOUT URANUS

SIZE: IT'S BIG. BUT LIKE, NOBODY KNOWS EXACKLY HOW BIG CAUSE, LIKE, IF YOU TRY TO MEASURE IT, THE GRAVITY SUCKS YOU INTO URANUS. URANUS. HUH HUH HUH HUH HUH. M HEH HEH HEH. THAT'S LIKE THE OPPOSITE AS ON EARTH. CAUSE LIKE HERE ON EARTH, WHEN YOU'RE ON THE TOILET OR WHATEVER, GRAVITY SUCKS EVERYTHING <u>OUT</u> OF URANUS. HUH HUH HUH. HEH HEH M HEH HEH.

ATMOSPHERE: IT HAS THIS THING CALLED METHANE ON IT, WHICH DARIA TOLD US COMES FROM FARTING. SO IT'S LIKE, CALLED THE SBD PLANET. THAT'S JUST ITS NICKNAME, THOUGH.

NAME: THE BOOK SAYS IT'S NAMED FOR THIS GREEK DUDE. RIGHT.

MOONS AND RINGS: THERE'S MOONS AND RINGS ON URANUS. HUH HUH HUH HUH. HEH HEH M. JUST LIKE BEAVIS'S MOM. IT'S LIKE, SOMETIMES, IF YOU LOOK AT HER WHEN SHE'S ASLEEP, LIKE AT AROUND NOON, AND THE SHEETS ARE ALL OVER THE PLACE, SHE'LL BE MOONING YOU, HUH HUH. THEN BEAVIS GETS ALL PISSED, HUH HUH. AND THEN, ALL THOSE DUDES SHE KNOWS, SHE SAYS THEY'RE HER COUSINS. BUT THEY GIVE HER RINGS AND STUFF. THEN SHE GIVES THE RINGS TO THE DUDE AT THE PAWN SHOP AND SHE GOES OUT AND LIKE, BUYS SOME HAIR SPRAY OR LIKE GOVERMENT CHEESE OR WHATEVER. BEAVIS'S MOM HAS A LOT IN COMMON WITH URANUS. URANUS. HUH HUH HUH HUH HUH HUH. HEH HEH HEH HEH M HEH HEH. WAIT. WAIT. SHUT UP, BUTT-HEAD. FARTKNOCKER.

PRACTICE SENTENCES:
URANUS IS A DARK AND MYSTERIOUS PLACE. HUH HUH HUH HUH HUH.
I DON'T THINK CIVILIANIZED PEOPLE WILL EVER GO TO URANUS. HEH HEH HEH. HEH.
BEAVIS, IF YOU PISS ME OFF ONE MORE TIME I'M GOING TO RIP URANUS IN HALF. HUH HUH.
BUZZCUT SUCKS.

Patrick Henry, Patriot and Orifice

THE FONDLING FATHERS WHO STARTED THIS COUNTRY SPENT ALL THEIR TIME GIVING SPEECHES, BUT THE GREATEST ORIFICE OF THEM ALL WAS PATRICK HENRY. HE COULD TALK ABOUT ANYTHING -- CHICKS, DOGS, YOUR WEINER, WHY THE WORLD SUCKS. YOU KNOW, IMPORTANT STUFF.

PATRICK HENRY LOVED THE SOUND OF HIS OWN VOICE. AND HE LOVED THE SOUND OF HIS OWN BUTT. THAT'S BECAUSE HE ATE LOTS OF BEAN BURRITOS. EVERYWHERE HE WENT, YOU COULD HEAR HIM TALKING AND FARTING, TALKING AND FARTING. HE TALKED SO MUCH AND FARTED SO MUCH, HE MADE LIKE UH...A *REPUTATION*.

SO ONE DAY ALL THE FONDLING FATHERS LIKE GEORGE WASHING AND ABRAHAM LINCOLN AND THE JEFFERSONS WERE STANDING AROUND TALKING ABOUT WHAT KIND OF COUNTRY THIS SHOULD BE. SOME WANTED A DEMONOCRACY, WHERE EVERYONE COULD DO WHAT THEY WANT LIKE IT SAYS ON THE *STATUE OF LIBERTY*. OTHERS WANTED A *DORKOCRACY*, HUH HUH, WHERE ONE ASSWIPE RUNS EVERYTHING LIKE IN BUZZCUT'S CLASS.

FINALLY PATRICK HENRY GOT UP AND MADE A FAMOUS SPEECH. HE SAID, "GIVE ME LIBERTY OR PULL MY FINGER!" SO EVERYONE CHOSE LIBERTY BECAUSE THEY DIDN'T WANT TO PULL PATRICK HENRY'S FINGER AND RELEASE SOME OF THAT REPUTATION.

BILLY THE KID'S VIRGIN

"PULL MY FINGER" HAS BEEN PLAYED THRU THE AGES BY PEOPLE OF MANY LANDS AND LANGUAGES. THAT IS BECAUSE YOU DON'T HAVE TO BE, LIKE, DEVELOPED TO PLAY IT. BEAVIS COULD FART BEFORE HE COULD WALK.

YEAH, HEH HEH. I COULD DUMP, TOO.

IN MEXICO THEY SAY, "PULL MY FINGER, ÉSE." IN FRANCE THEY SAY, "POOL MY FEENGER, SHEREE." IN GERMANY THEY SAY, "YA! YA! PULL MY FINGER! YA! YA!" HUH HUH. HUH HUH. ASSWIPES.

SOME PEOPLE PLAY DIFFERENT VIRGINS OF THE GAME. BILLY THE KID LIVED IN THE OLD WEST AND HE INVENTED AN INTERESTING VIRGIN. HE'D GO UP TO SOME DUDE ON THE STREET AND SAY, "PULL MY FINGER." AND WHEN THE GUY DID, BILLY FILLED HIM FULL OF LEAD. THAT WAS COOL. EVENTUALLY BILLY THE KID WAS KILLED BY PAT GARRETT. ACCORDING TO HYSTERIANS, GARRETT USED TWO FINGERS.

BEAVIS IN THE LIBRARY

BEAVIS IS PRETTY FUNNY. ONE DAY BEAVIS AND ME HAD TO GO TO THE SCHOOL LIBRARY BECAUSE WE FORGOT TO STAY HOME.

WHILE WE WERE AT THE LIBRARY, OUR TEACHER MRS. DICKEY, HUH HUH, GOT MAD AT THE CLASS CAUSE IT WAS HER PERIOD. SHE SAID, "EVERYBODY SHUT UP!"

SO THEN IT WAS QUIET FOR A WHILE. THEN BEAVIS SAID, "PULL MY FINGER." I PULLED HIS FINGER AND HE LET A REAL LOUD FART. IT WAS REALLY COOL.

YOU'RE PRETTY FUNNY, BEAVIS.

YEAH, HEH HEH, I KNOW. REMEMBER THAT TIME I CUT ONE IN THE LIBRARY?

IF WE MADE, LIKE, A VIDEO

ABOUT 108% OF ALL VIDEOS SUCK, NO MATTER HOW LOUD YOU TURN UP THE TV. THAT'S BECAUSE LIKE MOST PEOPLE DON'T KNOW HOW TO DO IT RIGHT. THEY'RE TOO BUSY LIKE, MAKING VIDEOS THAT ARE LIKE SPOSED TO

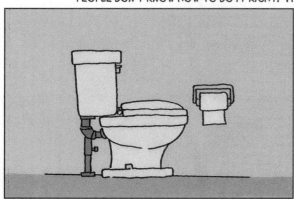

1. THE INTRODUCTION. LIKE THE INTRODUCTION HAS TO BE SO COOL THAT PEOPLE WATCH THE REST OF THE VIDEO. LIKE, WE'D PROBLY PUT A TOILET IN THE INTRODUCTION. AND THAT WAY PEOPLE WOULD GO, "UH, THIS LOOKS COOL. I WONDER IF THEY'RE GONNA FLUSH IT. HEY, WHAT IF A FAT GUY SITS ON IT? INSTRESTING. I GUESS I'LL JUST KEEP WATCHING TO SEE WHAT HAPPENS."

2. EXPLOSION. ANY TIME IS THE RIGHT TIME FOR AN EXPLOSION. IT WOULD BE COOL TO SEE LIKE A GUY ON A MOTORCYCLE EXPLODE. BUT LIKE, THE TV COMPANIES GET WUSSY ABOUT SHOWING THAT KIND OF STUFF, CAUSE THEY'RE AFRAID PEOPLE WILL DO IT? SO, LIKE, AS A COMPROMISE, JUST EXPLODE THE GUY AND LEAVE THE MOTORCYCLE ALONE.

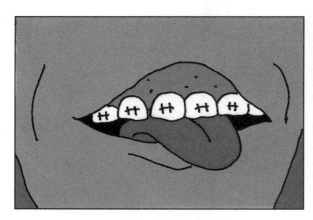

5. UH, LIKE, IF WE HAD FANS, THEY'D PROBLY BE MOSTLY CHICKS. HUH HUH. SO LIKE, WE'D NEED TO PUT SOME PICTURES OF ME IN THE VIDEO. LIKE, I THINK IT'D BE GOOD TO HAVE A CLOSEUP OF MY MOUTH AND TONGUE, HUH HUH. THAT'S LIKE ONE OF THE PARTS OF MY BODY THAT TURNS CHICKS ON THE MOST, HUH HUH HUH.

6. UM, THIS IS A GOOD PLACE FOR ANOTHER EXPLOSION. IF YOU ONLY HAVE ONE EXPLOSION, YOU CAN PUT IT ANYWHERE, CAUSE YOUR VIDEO WILL PROBLY SUCK. BUT IF YOU HAVE MORE THAN ONE, DON'T PUT 'EM ALL AT THE BEGINNING, OR PEOPLE'LL FEEL GYPPED. AND LIKE, IN A LOT OF VIDEOS, THEY JUST BLOW UP BUILDINGS AND STUFF, WITH LIKE A TOTAL DISREGARD FOR INCLUDING HUMAN LIFE. THAT WON'T BE A PROBLEM IN OUR VIDEO, HEH HEH.

MEAN SOMETHING. BUT ALL A VIDEO'S SPOSED TO MEAN IS THAT TV DOESN'T SUCK FOR THREE MINUTES. SO LIKE, WE'VE MADE IT SIMPLE FOR PEOPLE TO DO A COOL VIDEO. SPECIALLY CAUSE IT STARS US.

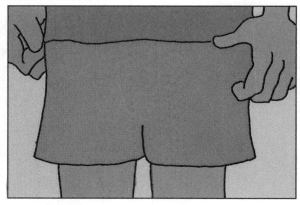

3. CHICKS REALLY GIVE A VIDEO SOMETHING, AND THAT SOMETHING IS CHICKS. CERTAIN KINDS OF DANCING CHICKS ARE GOOD TO HAVE IN A VIDEO. BUT ONLY CERTAIN KINDS. HUH HUH. SLUTS, MOSTLY. UH, IF YOU HAVE LIKE QUESTIONS, ME AND BEAVIS CAN PERSONALLY CHECK OUT EACH CHICK TO MAKE SURE SHE'S THE RIGHT KIND OF DANCING CHICK, HUH HUH.

4. UM, LIKE, A VIDEO IS FOR ALL PEOPLE TO ENJOY, BUT MOSTLY IT'S FOR THE FANS, HEH HEH. SO LIKE, SINCE WE'RE THE STARS, WE WANNA SHOW US IN WAYS WE'VE NEVER BEEN SEEN BEFORE. LIKE A GIANT CLOSEUP OF MY CROTCH WOULD BE PRETTY COOL. HEH HEH. THEY'D BE LIKE, "I'LL BE DAMNED. NEVER SAW THAT BEFORE." HEH HEH.

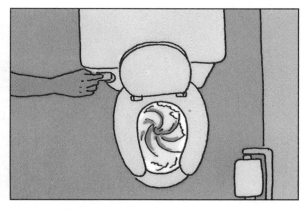

7. IF YOUR SONG'S ABOUT LOVE, YOU SHOULD PROBLY SYMBOLIZE THAT WITH SOME PICTURES OF PEOPLE DOING IT, HUH HUH. PROBLY ME AND ONE OF THE DANCER CHICKS ARE DOING IT. OR LIKE, WE'RE JUST ABOUT TO DO IT. YOU CAN TELL WE'RE JUST ABOUT TO CAUSE SHE HASN'T LEFT THE ROOM YET. HUH HUH. SHE WANTS ME.

8. LIKE, AT THE END OF THE VIDEO, YOU'D PROBLY WANNA PUT THE TOILET BACK IN AGAIN, BECAUSE RIGHT NOW EVERYBODY'S GOING, HEY, WHATEVER HAPPENED TO THAT TOILET. AND YOU'D GO, FUNNY YOU SHOULD ASK. IT'S BEING FLUSHED, HEH HEH. THAT'S OUR STORY, THANKS VERY MUCH. HEH HEH.

HUH HUH. I GUESS NOW IT'S TIME TO PICK A COOL SONG TO GO WITH THE VIDEO.

NO WAY! A SONG WOULD, LIKE, RUIN IT.

OH YEAH. VIDEOS RULE. SONGS SUCK.

WW HOW TO LIKE WORK AT BURGER WORLD

THEY SAY THAT WORKING AT THE WORLD IS SPOSED TO BE LIKE, UH, CHALLENGING OR SOME-
THING. BUT LIKE, WHAT THEY DON'T TELL YOU IS THAT IT'S LIKE A JOB.

So LIKE IF YOU'RE WORKING AT THE WORLD, HERE'S SOME TIPS TO GET THROUGH
YOUR SHIFT SO YOU CAN GET PAID. THEN YOU CAN GO BUY SOME REAL FOOD, LIKE NACHOS.

PUNCHING IN
UH, HUH HUH. GET IT?

Rong ~~Right~~ Way

Cool Way

Hi, welcome to Burger World.
How may I ~~help~~ you today?

40

HUH HUH HUH HUH.
YOU'RE OLD.

GREETING THE CUSTOMER
UH, LIKE CUSTOMERS
ARE ALWAYS AROUND
TRYING TO MESS UP
YOUR DAY. SO IT'S LIKE
IMPORTANT THAT THE
CUSTOMER GETS A REAL
CLEAR IDEA OF WHAT
TO EXPECT. IT'S LIKE
TREAT THEM THE WAY
YOU WANT THEM TO
TREAT YOU IF YOU LIKE
SUCKED OR SOMETHING.

MAKING THE CUSTOMER GO AWAY

THEY KEEP TELLING YOU THAT IT'S LIKE IMPORTANT FOR THE WORLD TO LIKE LIVE UP TO THE NAME "FAST FOOD," EVEN THOUGH FAST FOOD ISN'T EVEN IN THE NAME. ASSWIPES. SO YOU SHOULD MAKE THEM WANT TO LIKE LEAVE FAST, HUH HUH.

TALK ABOUT GROSS STUFF.

SCREW UP THE ORDER.

DON'T TAKE ANY CRAP FROM PEOPLE.

HANDLING THE MEAT, HUH HUH

LIKE, HANDLING THE MEAT IS FUN, HEH HEH. IT'S LIKE, TIME TO HANDLE THE MEAT, I'M GOING ON BREAK. BUT ALWAYS WASH YOUR HANDS AFTER YOU DO IT.

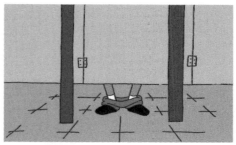

USING THE GRILL AND STUFF

WITHOUT THE GRILL, BURGER WORLD WOULD JUST BE, LIKE, UH, WORLD. BUT IT'S NOT JUST LIKE A GRILL OR SOMETHING. IT'S, UH, A BIG FLAT HOT THING YOU CAN COOK CRAP ON TOO.

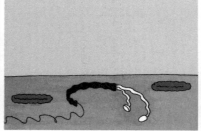

CHECK TO SEE IF THE GRILL IS HOT. A GOOD WAY IS TO TELL BEAVIS THAT IF HE LOOKS REAL CLOSE HE CAN SEE A NAKED CHICK IN THE GREASE.

IT'S FUN TO FRY THE HEADSET CAUSE PEOPLE THINK IT'S LIKE STATIC, HUH HUH.

IF YOU'RE MELTING SOMETHING PLASTIC, LIKE SOMEBODY'S CREDIT CARD, DON'T LET IT BURN UNLESS YOUR SUPERVISOR'S TOO FAR AWAY TO SMELL IT.

DEALING WITH LEFTOVERS

BURGER FRISBEE

F-TIPS

SHAKE GLUE

FIRST AID

LIKE, IF SOMEBODY HURTS THEMSELVES ON THE GRILL OR SOMETHING, TELL THEM TO QUIT SCREWING AROUND AND GET BACK TO WORK. IF THEY BLEED ON THE FOOD AND STUFF, TELL PEOPLE IT'S LIKE A NEW KETCHUP WE'RE TESTING OR SOMETHING.

CLEANING THE BATHROOMS

IT'S COOL TO CLEAN THE BATHROOMS CAUSE, LIKE, YOU CAN WATCH PEOPLE COME IN AND TRY TO PINCH A LOAF AND DRAIN THEIR WEINERS AND STUFF AND THEY LIKE, GET NERVOUS. TRY TO LIKE RELAX THEM BY SAYING, "HEY, IT'S COOL, PINCH YOUR LOAF IN PEACE." IF NOBODY COMES IN, THOUGH, YOU CAN JUST SLEEP AND STUFF.

PUNCHING OUT

HUH HUH. I BET YOU GET IT NOW.

VANDALISM – THESE ARE THOSE GUYS. THE ONES WHO PRAY ON TV. THE TV VANDALIST GUYS. THEY TELL YOU THAT THEY WANT YOU TO BECOME LIKE A FULL FAITH PARTNER IN THE MINISTRY FOUNDATION, AND THEN THEY CRY, SO YOU SEND THEM MONEY, AND THEN THE TV VANDALIST GETS YOU INTO HEAVEN. HE'S LIKE A BOUNCER OR SOMETHING. BUT CAN TV VANDALISM GET THOSE DUDES INTO HEAVEN WHO, UH, EGGED ANDERSON'S HOUSE LAST NIGHT? HUH HUH. THAT'S WHERE LIKE FAITH OR SOMETHING COMES IN, DUDE.

VEGETABLES – THESE ARE THOSE THINGS THEY SAY YOU'RE SPOSED TO EAT. BUT LIKE, IF THEY'RE NOT ON THE BURGER WORLD MENU, HOW IMPORTANT CAN THEY BE? THE BEST THING TO DO WITH VEGETABLES IS THROW THEM AT CITY BUSES AND ANDERSON.

VIETMOM – VIETMOM IS A COUNTRY IN CHINA, BUT IT'S ALSO A WAR. AND CAUSE WE HAD IT DURING THE 60s, THE ONLY SOLDIERS WE COULD GET WERE HIPPIES AND STUFF, SO NATURALLY WE GOT OUR ASS KICKED. BUT THEN WE INVENTED RAMBO, AND HE WENT BACK AND WON THE WAR, AND IT WAS CALLED OPERATION DESERT NAM. SO EVEN THOUGH WE REALLY WON, SOMETIMES WE CALL IT A TIE TO MAKE THE PEOPLE IN VIETMOM FEEL BETTER.

VIRGIN – HUH HUH HUH HUH HUH. THIS IS LIKE A DUDE OR A CHICK WHO'S NEVER DONE IT. FOR MORE INFORMATION, SEE BEAVIS.

WAR OF THE WORLDS – THIS IS A WAR THAT HAPPENED A LONG TIME AGO, WHEN ANDERSON WAS A YOUNG DUDE. LIKE, A HUNDRED POUNDS AGO, OR SOMETHING. SO WHAT HAPPENED WAS, THE CHINESE BOMBED PEARL HARBOR, AND SO WE HAD TO FIGHT BOTH THE GERMANS AND THE NAZIS. THEN THERE WAS D-DAY, AND THEY SAY THIS DUDE RAN AROUND SAYING, "THE BRITISH ARE COMING!" BUT HE PROBLY WASN'T ANDERSON CAUSE THE DUDE NEVER SAID ANYTHING ABOUT WANTING A BEER.

WEDGIE – THERE ARE LIKE DIFFERENT KINDS OF WEDGIES. THERE'S LIKE THE NORMAL EVERYDAY WEDGIE, LIKE WHEN BEAVIS PISSES YOU OFF FOR NO REASON. THEN THERE'S LIKE THE FIRST-CLASS WEDGIE, LIKE THE ONES THE SENIORS GIVE ON TORTURE DAY, AND YOU HAVE TO LIKE WALK AROUND WITH IT ALL DAY OR GET AN ATOMIC WEDGIE, WHICH REALLY DESERVES ITS OWN DEFINITION.

WEDGIE, ATOMIC – HEH HEH. WHEN, LIKE, BUTT-HEAD SAYS HE CAN KICK TODD'S ASS, AND TODD HEARS HIM? AND WHEN YOU SEE BUTT-HEAD A LITTLE LATER HANGING FROM THE TOP OF A LOCKER BY HIS UNDERWEAR? AND HE'S TALKING ALL CHOKED UP? THAT'S LIKE AN ATOMIC WEDGIE.

WEINER – THERE'S LIKE TWO DIFFERENT MEANINGS FOR THIS WORD, WHICH LIKE, PROVES HOW MESSED UP THE ENGLISH LANGUAGE IS. BUT THE DEFINITION FOR WEINER THAT MOST PEOPLE USE IS UH, HUH HUH HUH, YOUR THING. THE OTHER MEANING IS HARDLY EVER USED ANYMORE BUT, LIKE, THEY USED TO SAY A WEINER WAS A HOT DOG. ONE TIME STEWART'S DAD WAS GRILLING STUFF AND HE GOES, "WHO WANTS A WEINIE?" AND LIKE, STEWART WENT, "ME!" THAT WHOLE FAMILY'S LIKE, MESSED UP.

WOOD – WOOD IS THE BEST PART ABOUT BEING A DUDE, PRACTICALLY. IT'S LIKE, YOU COULD TAKE AWAY ALL MY MONEY AND MY CLOTHES AND MY TV, AND I'D PROBLY LIVE. BUT IF YOU TOOK AWAY MY WOOD, IT'S LIKE, WHY WOULD I EVEN WANT TO?

WUSS – THIS IS A PERSON WHO'S LIKE SO PATHETIC AND WEAK AND SORRY THAT IF YOU GAVE HIM A BASEBALL BAT AND LIKE, A BIG CHAIN WITH SPIKES IN IT, AND SOME KNIVES, AND THEN YOU PUT HIM IN A LITTLE TINY ROOM WITH THAT DUDE FROM THE B-52s, THE B-52 DUDE WOULD STILL KICK HIS ASS. HUH HUH. FOR MORE INFORMATION, WRITE TO BEAVIS, 1515 WUSSY AVENUE, WUSSBURG, WUSSYLVANIA, 029WUSS4. HUH HUH.

STONEHEDGE
CAUSE EVERYBODY WONDERS WHAT THE HELL IT IS. LIKE, I WONDER WHAT KIND OF STUPID DILLHOLE WOULD HAUL A BUNCH OF ROCKS UP A HILL AND LIKE, NOT GET PAID CAUSE THEY DIDN'T INVENT MONEY YET? HEY, THAT MAKES STONEHEDGE TWO WONDERS.

THE GREAT WALL OF CHINA
UHHH, PINK FLOYD MADE A PRETTY COOL MOVIE ABOUT IT. BUT I GUESS THEY TORE IT DOWN AT SOME CONCERT IN GERMONEY.

WUNDER BREAD
LIKE, YOU CAN SQUEEZE IT AND WONDER IF THAT'S WHAT A CHICK FEELS LIKE.

BEAVIS
I WONDER IF HE'S EVER GONNA GET ANY! HUH HUH HUH.

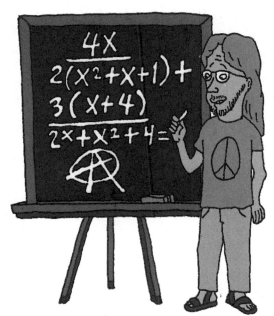

ALGEBRA
HUH HUH HUH HUH HUH.

CIRCLES
THOSE CIRCLES THAT LED ZEPLIN PUT IN FIELDS. THOSE STUPID FARMERS DON'T EVEN KNOW WHO'S PUTTING THEM THERE! WHAT A BUNCH OF DUMBASSES!

STEVIE WONDER
HE CAN, LIKE, DEFECT BULLETS WITH HIS MAGIC BRACES.

YO! BOOKWORM!

If you love this Beavis and Butt-head property, you'll like some of the other titles available from MTV Books! Check it out:

* *

The Real World 3. All the inside facts, photos, and bios about the lovable crew of Lombard Street loonies. Special pull-out recipe section. **12.95**

* * * * * * * * * * * * * * * * * * * *

Free Your Mind Fashion. Spend a little time with some straight-talking, forward-thinking individualists who are wearing this year's <u>hottest</u> must-have clothes -- while treating everyone they meet as complete equals! **10.95**

* * * * * * * * * * * * * * * * * * * *

The Making of the President 1992. MTV executives gave journalist George Stephanopoulos complete access to files, memos and storyboards to reveal for the first time how MTV viewers elected Bill Clinton president, and why what the other 95 percent of the electorate did doesn't factor in. Includes coupon for $3.00 off Nickelodeon's "The Making of the President 2004." **9.95**

* *

VH-1's Great Chardonnays Of The 80s. A bottle of Stag's Leap '86, Michael Bolton, and thou...and other recipes for vintage pleasure. **14.95**

* * * * * * * * * * * * * * * * * * * *

The Real World 2. The story of a group of people trying to make it in a town they call the City of Angels. Inside photos, facts, and bios. **Was 12.95, now 8.95!**

* *

America's Watersheds: An Eco-Historical Overview. By Eric Nies. In his previously unpublished doctoral dissertation, the host of *MTV's The Grind* takes a look at the neglected problem of water supply, and sounds a sobering warning about North America's over-taxed aquifer system. Maps, notes, extensive bibliography. **39.95**

* *

Learn It Or Leave It: MTV's Guide To American History. Did you know the Civil War was fought on <u>American</u> soil? Fascinating facts like these compiled by Tabitha Soren for the generation about to run the planet's most powerful country. **10.95**

* * * * * * * * * * * * * * * * * * * *

Gangstas Without Honor. Learn about hip-hop artists who speak the uncomfortable truths about the inequities of the system. This is the book "the Man" doesn't want you to read. Plus, special contest where <u>you</u> can win a trip to Hollywood! With a foreword by Demi Moore. **8.95**

* * * * * * * * * * * * * * * * * * * *

Mouse of Style. Cindy Crawford's delightful children's fable about a little rodent who wouldn't wear the same thing twice. Illustrated by Todd Oldham's nephew. **5.95**

* * * * * * * * * * * * * *

Kurt on Kurt. They never met. They never spoke. But respected MTV news anchor Kurt Loder believes that if he had gotten to know Kurt Cobain, his reminiscences would go a little something like this. **12.95**

* * * * * * * * * * * * * *

The Real World. All about the original group—with inside bios, facts, and photos—and the show that started a phenomenon. **Was 8.95, now 3.95!**

* *

Available at bookstores or where other fine media are sold.